Maurice O'Connor Morris

Rambles in the Rocky Mountains

with a visit to the gold fields of Colorado

Maurice O'Connor Morris

Rambles in the Rocky Mountains
with a visit to the gold fields of Colorado

ISBN/EAN: 9783337287344

Printed in Europe, USA, Canada, Australia, Japan

Cover: Foto ©Andreas Hilbeck / pixelio.de

More available books at **www.hansebooks.com**

RAMBLES

IN THE

ROCKY MOUNTAINS:

WITH A VISIT TO THE

GOLD FIELDS OF COLORADO.

BY

MAURICE O'CONNOR MORRIS,

LATE DEPUTY POSTMASTER-GENERAL OF JAMAICA.

LONDON:

SMITH, ELDER AND CO., 65, CORNHILL.

1864.

PREFACE.

In offering to the Public these extracts from a journal kept for the perusal of a few friends, and meant to supplement private letters, I feel that an apology is due for many insertions and omissions, which, under different circumstances, would have been as inadmissible as inexcusable. The region, however, through which my rambles have led me possesses so much of interest and importance in an age which may in some respects—though Janus' shrine yawns so terribly open—be described as a golden one, and which to us "Britishers" is pre-eminently so, that I trust the many imperfections of these "Recollections" will be pardoned, in consideration of their introduction to a territory which to the great mass of readers in Eng-

land is as imperfectly known as Timbuctoo or the
country of the "Fanns."

As an instance of the small amount of geographical
knowledge of Colorado possessed by even tolerably
well-informed persons, I may mention that a very
eminent banking firm of the metropolis addressed a
letter to me while there superscribed thus :—

Denver, Nova Scotia ;

while a distinguished barrister, my learned friend
and correspondent, would persist in locating Denver
in the State of Kansas. And, indeed, considering
the little light shed on this quarter of the globe by
the maps in ordinary use, and the wonderful and
almost portentous growth of this remote region, to
which the ocean has washed no foreigners, as in
Australia and California, this Cimmerian darkness is
not surprising. A spot of this earth, however, which
boasts—how truly I have no exact means of ascertaining—of having added twenty-five millions of
dollars' worth in bullion during the past year to
the national wealth of the Federal States, under
circumstances little favourable to development, and
with most inadequate resources of labour and capital,

cannot long remain ignored; more especially when, in addition to its auriferous wealth, Nature has endowed it with a store of minerals comprising almost every species known, in great affluence, and a climate favourable to their exploration, with a soil which, properly cultivated, is capable of great results.

I therefore hope that in the hurried descriptions of things seen *obiter*, I may at least claim the merit, *si qua est ea gloria*, of drawing attention to a subject of some general interest hitherto unexplored; while, in explanation of any and all major and minor errors of style, grammar, history, or physiology, let me confess that my faculties for writing are sensibly affected by the *genius loci*, and especially by the means and appliances for the purpose within reach, and that these pages had to be transcribed for the most part in the uncongenial atmosphere of a prophet's chamber-like bed-room in Denver, nearly as large as a ship's cabin, but too small for such a superfluity as a table, and where a washing-stand of small proportions, like Goldsmith's chest of drawers, was forced for the nonce a double debt to pay: under which untoward circumstances my sheets were prepared for the post, with a haste very unworthy of the subject; the result of which, in the language of rebuked officials writing to their senior pundits of "the" department, "I acknowledge and regret."

RAMBLES

IN THE

ROCKY MOUNTAINS.

CHAPTER I.

Westward the course of empire holds its sway.

To the West ! to the West ! to the land of the Free !
Where the mighty Missouri rolls on to the sea, &c.

BOTH words and air had somehow for a long time
been associated in my mind with America, and
seemed to be incorporated with the very essence and
idea of that great country; and yet, like the national
anthem, which boasts that the "Star-spangled banner
in triumph shall wave on the home of the free and
the land of the brave," (or, as a sarcastic friend of
mine parodied the latter line into the "Home of the
free and the land of the slave,") who will be bold
enough to assert that these inspiring words have not

1

utterly lost their significance : indeed, to those who
knew and appreciated their real meaning in times
gone by, they can only serve now to embitter
memory.   The poet's crown of sorrow is, " The
remembering happier things."

But I am not going to enter into a diagnosis of
the social and political maladies of this vast country,
sick with civil strife, or indulge in Jeremiads for
the present condition of affairs, or vaticinations of
gloom which political charlatans on both sides of
the Atlantic are daily pouring forth.   The facts are
melancholy enough, God knows, without forestalling
the woes to come, or discounting future miseries at
compound interest.   And methinks the feelings of
every Englishman should be more in unison with
those of the heart-sore king when he exclaimed—

> Oh, my poor country, sick with civil broils
> If that my care could not contain thy riot,
> What wilt thou do now riot is thy care ?

For, separated as they are by the " unsociable
ocean "—as Horace, born before the Cunard era,
declared it to be—and by the rivalries and jealousies
naturally incident to two great competing powers,
and even still more by the traditions and legacies of
the revolutionary wars, who can say that England and
America are not more inseparably linked together by

ties which, extending far back into the past, and increasing daily with the march of civilization, embrace a future as distant as the mind can grasp, than any other two nations in this universe. Ties of blood, language, literature, commerce, and by the less material, though not less puissant, bond of spiritual communion.

To the West, then, I " concluded," as our cousins express such a determination, to proceed; and being in the empire city of New York, the only " embarras du choix " was the selection of the best route. No less than three main lines contend for the traveller's patronage, each offering some special attraction; and as they vary but little in time and accommodations, one is puzzled to which terminus or dépôt (pronounced usually as a nigger lad learning geography might, the chief river of Italy—De-Po,) one should go. My difficulties were, however, relieved by finding a friend who had selected the Erie line, and as I was already familiar with the best portions of what one may call the " Northern route " via Albany, Detroit, &c., and of the " Pennsylvania Central," I gladly hailed the chance of an extremely pleasant compagnon de voyage. We left Jersey City,—the Birkenhead of New York,—about five o'clock P. M., on the Tuesday, and travelling incessantly night and day, reached

St. Louis, the metropolis (not capital) of the great
state of Missouri, about two o'clock A.M. on the
Friday morning, a few hours behind time.

In America a tourist may draw conclusions from
railway travelling, which in England would be very
erroneous; for in the former the railway is the pioneer
of all progress. Civilization and settlements follow
it, and seem to cling close to it for protection.
Towns and villages grow round it, and to show their
gratitude, welcome it daily through their best streets,
as they used to welcome the daily stage in the old
country, in the merry days of the road. And, indeed, in most parts of the recently settled districts,
civilization is bounded by the railway margin more
or less wide; whereas in the older civilization of
Europe, and England specially, railways had to skirt
towns and villages, and to hide their heads in such
neighbourhoods, either by tunnels or embankments,
completely obscuring the view; or else they emerged
from a town on a line with the chimney pots, and
through the dirtiest of slums—regarded even then as
rather a nuisance : so that in reality, between the
pace made by the engine,—usually rather double
the American average—and the obstacles to sight
presented by embankments, fences, &c., one does
not get a good idea of the country travelled through

in England, much less of what lies beyond the horizon of your carriage. In America the sample seen from your cars may be considered a fair one.

I confess I was much disappointed in the aspect of Nature, for most of the distance between Jersey City and Erie, on the shore of the great lake of that name, the land seemed barren and unimproved to a degree, capable of but little, and that little not accomplished; the farming was bad and backward, with stumps of several feet in height dotting the fields everywhere, and, were it not for the fine water-power afforded by numerous streams, and the facilities for lumbering, all this district seemed to present no allurements to the settler. Once in Ohio, however, the scene changes. Rich fields of large dimensions, and mathematically square, generally clear of stumps, and enclosed with solid posts and rails, and shaded by fine timber, meet the eye on each side of the track, and an air of comfort and wealth pervades everything. Great rivers, such as the Wabash, the Ohio, and the Miami, seem to glide along lazily as if they wished to linger amid the luxuriance they have helped to create; while the "Old Kentucky shore" seems a perfect paradise of high farming and agricultural wealth, looking from the opposite side of the

Ohio, like one vast park stretching away for miles in beautiful undulations.

Spite of the slight solace afforded by the " sleeping cars," in which, by paying an extra dollar,—or if you choose to take an upper shelf, half that sum,—you secure something very like a berth in a steamer, with all the apparatus for passing the night comfortably, the journey was beginning to feel very tedious, and I was not by any means sorry when the " cars " reached the eastern bank of the Mississippi, and the passengers transferred to an omnibus, and thence to a ferry steamer, were conveyed to their several destinations in the comparatively old city of St. Louis.

I had been told that this city suffered greatly from the war, but I must say that in my protracted stay there I saw no sign whatever of stagnation in business, or paralysis of any branch of trade. On the contrary, the hotels were so full that beds had to be bespoken some time in advance, while on the levée, a sort of terrace slanting down to the river's edge, commerce seemed as stirring and active as I have ever seen it. It is a curious sight for a stranger to view for the first time a large fleet of these huge river steamers, with their vast walking beams and stories rising one over the other, ranged

in a double line along the levée for considerably more
than a mile, their lofty funnels, yclept " smoke-
stacks," vandyked at the top, rising some thirty feet
into the air, and not, as in ocean-going steamers,
placed one after the other, but side by side, like a
tree with two stems.   True, many of these boats
were in the Government service, and were chartered
for the use of the troops in the Mississippi department, and "for Vicksburg" was somewhat osten-
tatiously paraded on some of their sides; still there
were a great number engaged in their usual legitimate commerce up the Mississippi and Missouri
rivers, and thence to the Ohio and other rivers.

Like almost every city (not absolutely of mushroom
growth), St. Louis has its old quartier, where the
streets rejoice in names of their own, and the new
one, where numbers are substituted for names; an
arrangement very convenient, no doubt, for the
traveller, but extremely unromantic, methinks, and
unfair to the inhabitants.   It always struck me, when
in New York, as a most levelling and mechanical
arrangement of bricks and mortar, and half the
grandeur of the fifth avenue seemed to me to evapo-
rate from its want of a more pleasing association of
ideas.   However, the streets in St. Louis are well laid
out, and broad, and, as the land rises to a con-

siderable elevation from the river, the drainage is admirable. Locomotion is aided by the street tramways, which convey the passenger any number of miles for the small sum of five cents, and withal smoothly enough, though very slowly.

There is no public building worth looking at, save the city hall, which has a fine dome, from which a very fine view of the city and its entourage is gained; but all have great pretensions to a respectable mediocrity, which in this country is something. Most denominations of religion have their temples, but the old faith of the first settlers seems to have taken deeper root than any of the others, if one may judge by the churches, convents, and schools which it has erected.

There is also a park, "the Lafayette," which is nicely situated in the upper regions of the city, and where pic-nics are usually held; but the trees, like those in the "Central" in New York, are quite young, and the grounds want care. I should not omit the "Mercantile Library," of which I was kindly given the run, which contains a gallery of rather indifferent pictures and a few pieces of sculpture, of which three, by the celebrated Miss Hosmer of steeple-chase renown in Rome, struck me as good :— a "Beatrice Cenci," an "Œnone," and a "Puck." It was a pleasant reading-room, and the "proprieties" were so strictly enforced, that a visit from the secretary in propriú, was the consequence of not removing your hat on entering the room. Don't it seem strange that our republican cousins should be such sticklers and martinets for their own code of etiquette, while they affect to hold so many of our conventionalities in contempt?

I should not omit mentioning among the public buildings, one which does and does not come under that category, the "Lindell Hotel," which has just been completed, though not yet opened to the public. It is a large square building, faced with yellow freestone, slightly ornamented; the sitting rooms have a stone-pillared gallery attached to them,—an immense resource in summer,—and altogether the accommodations are as perfect as I have ever seen, even in this land of hotels, when a man's smartness is gauged by his ability to work such an institution profitably. "Yes, sirree! Smith's a right smart sort o'chap, but he can't keep a hô-tel." I was proud to reflect that the architect of this huge and shapely pile, the largest on the Continent, was an Englishman!

While I was in St. Louis, the anniversary of "Camp Jackson," or the deliverance of Missouri

from something to their minds far worse than either
Popery or wooden shoes, was celebrated by the Fede-
ralist party; which seemed to contain a very large
proportion of the German, or, as called here, the
Dutch element. It seems that at the outbreak of
the war, the entire executive of the State of Missouri
was "tinctured" with southern "proclivities," and
had even gone so far as to invite Arkansas, a neighbouring State, to send troops to aid them in their
projects. However, they did not consider the pear
sufficiently ripe at the moment, and determined to
temporize and make further arrangements before
completing the "coup d'état." Meanwhile, a con-
vention of the people, which had been summoned
for some other purpose, hearing through their dele-
gates of these projects, proceeded forthwith to depose
the Secesh administration, and replaced it tempo-
rarily by a Republican cabinet. Volunteers were
raised and armed, and an attack was made upon
the rebels, who had encamped at Camp Jackson,
near the city, which ended in the rout and expul-
sion of the latter.

There can be no doubt that these vigorous
measures, which savoured rather of our quon-
dam seizure of the Danish fleet, kept Missouri
from openly seceding; and, as the Germans were

mainly instrumental in achieving this success, they are not by any means inclined to hide their light under a bushel, but swagger about considerably on the strength of being on the winning side this time.

St. Louis is the great out-fitting place for the far west, and the depôt for its produce. My friend who had now completed his preparations for spending a couple of months on the prairies, hunting buffalo, &c., and had made every arrangement for a comfortable commissariat, with tents, waggon, ambulance, spare ponies, and the hundred and one wants of camp existence here, took his departure, having been joined by his party from the east; and as I expected letters of importance, I had to remain per force in St. Louis, " varying, however, the monotony of the proceedings," as Mr. Cox remarks, by excursions in the vicinity in quest of snipe and duck: which I found, strange to say, very abundant, though April's moon's had nearly waned !

If it be true that a " watched pot never boils," I am sure a similar proposition anent letters is far more so, and of more general application. Talk of calling spirits from the vasty deep ! I am sure it were an easier process than eliciting answers in time from some correspondents ! So having exhausted my patience by waiting in vain, I determined to leave St. Louis at any rate; and as I heard I could, by pushing on to St. Joseph by rail, catch a steamer bound to the head waters of the Missouri, which had left only a few days in advance, I started off, intending to go up the river as far as the steamer could penetrate, namely, to Fort Benton, then cross over to Bannack City, visit the newly-discovered gold-diggings there, and return thence *via* Salt Lake, either to the eastern States by land, or *via* California and the Isthmus; from this I find a daily scratching of something in my pocket-book, which I may as well transfer to this page.

May 19*th.*—Left St. Louis by the North Missouri line at 2 A.M., having taken the precaution of obtaining a certificate from our excellent consul that I was a " Britisher," and that I only intended to turn the gun and rifle I carried against *feræ naturæ;* a certificate which had to be countersigned by the provost-marshal of that district. At Warrenton we stopped for an indifferent breakfast, and some apprehension having been entertained of guerillas (invariably termed " gorillas ") we found the line swarming with " *Lincoln's minions* "—fine rough-looking fellows, as different from my experience of Eastern volunteers as could be conceived.

At Macon City, which, to my eye, consisted of very few houses, and those mostly labelled "Hotel," we had to wait for "connection," or, as we should say, for the arrival of the branch line from Hannibal. In the meantime, I improved the occasion by conversing with a farmer of the neighbourhood, who was clad in the home-made Butternut cloth, very common in the West; so called from its colour, which is something darker than a stone ginger-beer bottle, and lighter than mahogany. I soon discovered he had "proclivities," and he asked me a great many questions about England. One of his interrogatories I must record. "Do you think folks here look natural?" By this he meant, Do they seem to you like your own people?

Soon after leaving Macon, we came on the genuine prairies, vast rolling plains covered with grass, in which farms were every now and then dotted about, fenced in by rails disposed zigzag fashion, and apparently producing good crops of wheat, oats, and Indian corn. These lands were beautifully wooded in places, and seemed full of prairie chickens, which kept rising as the train moved on. Some Illinois young ladies, who were paying a first visit to some friends near St. Joe, were much struck by the absence of school-houses and churches; this seemed to shock them very much, as they are such á prominent feature eastwards.

Some bits of these prairies reminded one of the Curragh of Kildare, as seen from the Southern and Western line, only there was more wood-land near, and no gorse. Arrived at St. Joe, I was spirited away by the persuasive eloquence of an Irish commissionaire to the " Patee House," a large brick building, some half mile at least from the town, and built in anticipation of the spread of building in that direction. This caravansery I reached about 12 o'clock P.M., and proceeded to a bedroom of ample dimensions; but, O horror ! I discovered the sheets were not by any means innocent of dirt : however, this is a trifle in the far West, so I had to pocket the insult to my feelings, and, after all, slept very well.

20th.—Made remonstrances about bed-clothes, and obtained what I wanted. Found, on inquiry, that the river was so low that the steamer I expected so long had not arrived as yet, and very probably might not be able to get up so high. Here was a regular break-up of all my plans; but as there was nothing for it but to wait patiently, I made up my mind to extract as much honey from St. Joe as it would yield. I had left a valuable watch in St. Louis

in the hands of a watchmaker, and thinking a watch
good company, and having regard to the uncertainty
of events in this State, I telegraphed for it, at the
heavy price of a dollar and some cents; this brought
me near the post-office and book store. I found
nothing in the latter but elementary treatises and
some novels, mostly reprints of English authors;
bought *Godolphin* and the *Oxonians*, by Bulwer,
who, I was informed by the vendor, was a good
author. Well, it is something to be *repandu* even
in St. Joe!

21st.—I have christened this place Κονιόπολις,
the City of Dust, for surely no Derby or Ascot road
knew such dust as the wind is raising everywhere.
The entire soil of this district, and I may say of the
entire West, so far as I have seen, is composed of
rich loam and sand; sometimes one predominates,
sometimes the other; and after a long spell of dry
weather it will be easily understood how a sirocco of
dust can be raised by sudden gusts.

Went to see a large encampment of Winnebago
Indians, who had been deported from Minnesota,
and were to be assigned some fresh lands in
Dacotah territory. It will be recollected that last
year the Sioux Indians massacred a number of
settlers in Minnesota, for which some thirty-six or

thirty-nine were hung; but these people were the foes of the Sioux, had no part or lot in their crime, yet a parental government were banishing them, simply as a measure of precaution, for fear of a collision between them and the whites, if they remained. Verily the red man has had hard measure meted out to him by his Uncle Sam!

When I was last in Washington, I went on a Sunday afternoon to the principal Episcopal Church, and, to my surprise, found the front seats occupied by sundry Indian chiefs, very respectably attired, who had come to Washington to see the President on business. Among the officiating clergy was an Indian, who, at the conclusion of the prayers, made a few very sensible remarks about his brethren, whom he then addressed in their own language. Then the two other clergymen delivered themselves of an oration a-piece, in which the main topic was the frightful injustice and oppression to which their red brother had been subjected by the Government; but they saw no hope of redress—no power to restrain the encroachment of the pioneers! Truly, if St. Paul's idea of the powers that be is a correct picture of what a Government should be, the executive of the United States falls very far short of the standard! The fact is, it is the popular will to hunt out the

Indians, and the Government cannot, if it would, say No. -

These Winnebagos appeared to me very peaceful and orderly; there were some very fine athletic men among them, and a few tolerable-looking squaws; but dirt was king among them all, and asserted his supremacy, though the river was flow-- ing within a few paces of them. There were a good many half-breeds among them, not unlike the mulattoes of the West Indies; but these seemed to have no higher instincts than their red relations, and were, to all intents and purposes, Indian. The fashionable game was a sort of *les graces*, only, instead of a hoop, a hollow ball was caught on the point of a stick, and then thrown back again. They had mat lodges instead of the usual skins. They were very strictly guarded, to prevent the introduction of the fatal fire-water, which fairly drives an Indian mad, and for which he would barter, perhaps, his soul. In the centre of their encampment, hung three fresh scalps which they had recently taken from the Sioux. It was amusing to watch the care they bestowed on these trophies; combing out the long locks with a solicitude and care which was probably never bestowed on them when their owners were " in the quick."

May 22nd.—Soft rain during the night has laid

2

the dust and cooled the intensely hot atmosphere. At breakfast I was waited on by a long scarecrow of a lad, and when I sent down a bit of what looked like fried leather, but which was called a beefsteak, he brought it up again, remarking, "If you don't like it, you may leave it." I called the head waiter, who was an Irishman evidently far above his business, and he informed me he was powerless, as even the boys had arms of one kind or another; but he nevertheless got me a better steak.

After breakfast, I watched an Irishman digging a foundation for his house, and as far as he penetrated, the soil was the richest black loam! Heavy rain in the evening, and lo! the city of dust becomes one of mud, black and soft, as I found to my cost; for going at night to inquire for my watch, which had not come, I got off the road, and found myself in much the same kind of country as that to which Tony Lumpkin introduced his London friends. There is gas in St. Joe, but it is not as yet used for lighting the streets! In my wrath I re-christened the city Πηλόπολις, or Mud Town.

While returning to the "Patee House" I heard strains of music, and saw a large building lighted up, and turned in to see the "divarshion," but found it was only an attempt at a ball, in which the maids of the hotel were the principal attraction. I " vamoosed " at once, and all but fell into the arms of a drunken soldier, who wanted to be very affectionate, and when I attempted to extricate myself from his hug, declared he would shoot me. He did not fire, however, but I have no doubt a very slight provocation, and a little light, might have induced him to do so. One captain and four civilians have been shot in brawls this week; all the troops carry revolvers, and the Colorado " boys," now in town, are said to be right " smart on the trigger."

23rd.—Finding that there is but slight prospect of the *Robert Campbell* steamer getting up the river in its present condition, I made up my mind to strike Westward, ho! and negotiated with a teamster who is going to Denver City, Colorado, to transport self and the slight impedimenta necessary for the apparently moderate sum of thirty dollars, which is to include provision viatica all the way; and considering that the distance is as near as possible 700 miles, and the time consumed *en route* is seldom less than twenty-five days, the moderation of the charge will, I think, be pretty self-evident. He has one four-mule team ready for the road, and a start is promised this evening, or to-morrow at daybreak. Accordingly, to be in readiness, I moved to the " Commercial Hotel," a sort of "Belle Sauvage" for the western teams, as it faces an enormous stable, or barn, as they call it here, full of mules, waggons, and the other paraphernalia for the road.

I learnt to-day a fact which I ought to have been aware of before, but was not, and that is that every man in the United States has to pay a poll-tax of one dollar and a half yearly for the maintenance of streets and roads, or commute it into two days' work on the roads. Judging from what I have seen of streets and roads, I cannot help thinking this large fund must be singularly misappropriated or jobbed!

The mule team is started at last, with our provisions and two passengers, and the driver ordered to go slowly, so as to enable us to catch him. But we never did.

Got up early, but found no sign of starting as yet. On inquiry I found that more passengers had come in, and insisted upon going in "this crowd," as any party is yclept in this part of the country. Feeling sure that, under the circumstances, no start could be effected for a few hours, I set out to have a look at the convent, a large brick building, which crowned the heights overlooking the town: for St. Joe is built on a slight bend of the Missouri, and the land rises into a semicircle of pretty high bluffs just above it. Of course I saw nothing at the convent but the exterior walls, and the place might have been tenantless for all I could see; but close by was a beautiful garden, paled in, though quite scaleable by any enterprising youth, and the palings were not so close but that the scene of Pyramus and Thisbe might have been enacted easily enough.

After taking a round of the bluffs, and surveying the beautiful rich country, with its farms and woodlands stretching away as far as the eye can see, I bethought me of church, and went into a modest temple which might be dedicated to Presbyterian, Baptist, or Methodist forms of worship. The sermon struck me as very forcible and good, and if the pronunciation was peculiar to English ears, the selection of words was extremely good.

By the way, I am not quite sure that the Americans have not got a great deal to say in favour of their pronunciation of some words, which I am inclined to think approximates considerably to the old English standard. I may instance the word "wound," which they pronounce as spelt; while we as if it were spelt "woond," making it rhyme with "tuned"—they with "sound;" then "deaf," which they render "deef," and "gaping," which they pronounce full, as all but Englishmen render the Latin *a* (and as most of our Shaksperian readers render that word, which occurs several times in his plays), and so on *ad infinitum*. At any rate, if the Americans murder the Queen's English in their own way, as *Punch* wittily dreaded they would when a collision in the *Trent* affair was imminent, I am sure we do so equally in ours; and certainly the letter "h" has a "better time of it" with them than with us: indeed, on the whole, I think that, man for man and woman for woman, the Americans speak better English than ourselves; though I believe our highest standard to be above theirs. They may, at any rate, claim to have produced in Lindley Murray the Quintillian of English grammar, and in Webster and Worcester the best lexicographers.

After the sermon a prayer extempore was made by a young assistant, which moved him to tears, and had the most spasmodic effect on a female member of the congregation, who went into hysterics forthwith, but was "let be" by her surroundings. After the prayer a hymn was sung by the pastor of the flock, and while singing he walked about shaking hands with most of the congregation in the forepart of the building. The effect was very curious, but it had a most tranquillizing influence on the troubled spirit

of the Niobe of this occasion. After these prelec-
tions, I turned towards the " Commercial," and
discovered that the start was postponed till Monday,
finally.

I have not said a word anent St. Joe, which, being
the second city in the State of Missouri, deserves it.
It is only a few years old, and yet it numbers about
9,000 inhabitants, boasts two vast hotels, and many
minor ones : the American idea being everywhere to
live in such establishments, and to dispense with all
domestic bothers. Being on the Missouri, it has the
advantage of the trade up and down that mighty
conduit, and is thus connected by water with
almost the entire continent for several thousand
miles ; while the North Missouri and Hannibal
and St. Joe lines, of which it is the terminus,
gives it the command of eastern and southern Missouri, Illinois, &c. ; then it has a short line of its
own to Atcheson, from which point the great Overland Stage Company starts for California.

It was a very flourishing place before the war,
and was fast rising into importance, but has been
under a blight ever since. Just now it is as completely under military occupation as any conquered
city need be : military law and police are in force,
and the dominant faction as completely lords it over

the beaten one as in the small Grecian States of which Thucydides has left us such an imperishable record. To hold certain opinions is to be an enemy, even though such opinions be carefully veiled; evidence is being continually hunted up to prove a "secession bias," and then woe to the unlucky holder of such unprofitable tenets! All his stock, at any rate, is considered fair game for confiscation. Having these lessons before their eyes, many of the farmers in the vicinity have sold off every horse and mule they possess, save perhaps one valueless animal for daily drudgery.

This state of things has given rise to bands of partisans, who sweep across the country, taking all they can, under the titles of "Guerillas," "Bushwackers," and "Jay-hawkers," and who, under pretence of taking sides with either party, commit frightful murders, and thus pay back old grudges and take vengeance for wrongs of long standing. Of course it would be unjust to blame either Federals or Confederates entirely for such a state of affairs. It is the natural result of a war such as desolates the continent just now, when carried into a State which is in the main friendly to the South, and which, as a slave State, believes its interests to be inseparable from theirs. I believe the

Federal troops are doing their best to repress these marauders; but local knowledge, and the vast distances, give the latter a great advantage. It is one of the most melancholy considerations incident to this war, that in the border States, such as Missouri, even if peace were proclaimed to-morrow, the *lex talionis* would probably for some time supplant the *jus civile*, and assassination would be very rife. Under these circumstances, it is not to be wondered at that land has greatly diminished in value, and that the peaceably disposed—who are, indeed, the great majority —are doing their best to realize their estates, and migrate further West.

This is not the privation to an American it would be to the citizen of any other country. These settlers have probably held their present tenures but for a short period; and though one would conceive that the fact of having redeemed a farm from the surrounding wilderness would endear it greatly to the settler, such is not generally the case, or at least not so much so but that a good per-centage will tempt him to sell at any time. He is above such a prejudice as having an inordinate weening for any one spot or earth, which he holds to be only worthy of a cat, or such an old fogy as Naboth the Jezreelite. Man never *is*, but only *to be* blessed. The West, with all, its

untold wealth, lies before him, and so his nomad
instincts prevail : he packs his worldly goods into
waggons, takes his flocks and his herds, and his
slaves, if he has any, with him, and thus goes prospecting for some new " location."

I should be very unwilling to credit the stories of
peculation and corruption which one hears of in all
departments, were it not for the revelations that the
Van Wyck Committee and other sources, in some
instances the public prints, have made; but, in any
case, I must say, like Herodotus, of these things :—
"I have heard, but have never seen them." It is
said àpropos of the confiscations of stock we have
heard of, that it was not at all unusual, when a contractor wanted to get a large number of animals, that
his first step would be to establish friendly relations
with the officers in command of the troops in the
neighbourhood ; then a raid would be concerted on
the stock of the "traitors," and a large haul made,
and thus the contractor would be enabled to fulfil
his engagement with his dear Uncle on the most
reasonable terms: the zeal of the officers not being
of course forgotten.

These little ebullitions have no doubt had the
effect of banishing many a "traitor" from Missouri ;
but there can be no doubt that there is an enormous

number of Southern sympathisers within its borders—
"galvanized" traitors, as they call them; and if any
success of Bragg's were to bring Price again with a
strong force into Missouri, I have no doubt he would
find a strong following. The Federals, indeed, are
walking over embers, "suppositos cineri doloso,"
which may blaze out into a frightful conflagration!

28th.—No signs of a start yet; soon, I discovered
the hitch—there were too many passengers for one
waggon, and too much luggage. Under these circumstances, I confess to an act of extreme weakness
and confidence, namely, lending our teamster
110 dollars towards a second waggon and pair
of mules or ponies; as I heard he was a man of
some substance and much probity, and, at any
rate, the ponies and waggons were always available
property in the far West.* Consequently, I was
allowed a voice in the selection of our means of
locomotion, and so picked out a second-hand spring
waggon, something like a break, which had, of
course, the usual awnings; and we hit on a pair
of stout ponies, which, I suppose, weighed about
sixteen cwt.

It is strange how in America horses are more estimated by their weight than by their shapes and action

* The principal was repaid in full on arriving at Denver.

as with us; still, it can't be denied that weight is a very essential element in slow draft. It is also curious to hear in the West, when one man describes another, how invariably he guesses at his weight in pounds. And now, this difficulty solved, for collecting the passengers, and packing the freight! I should mention that our other waggon was an ordinary one, not on springs, with the usual awnings, and the other pair of ponies were an extremely handsome round pair of little nags about 13·2, lighter than our last pair, and said to be capable of dragging St. Joe after them, if required; or, at any rate, a very fair load.

At last we got under weigh in very rough-and-ready style. The spring waggon—with four children and three women, and the "boss" driving, with its compliment of trunks and boxes, which formed the seats, and a tent lashed on behind—leading the van; we following in No. 2, five in number, but the luggage piled up fore and aft in such a way that there was nothing but a small well of some two and a half feet by three to sit in, perched on anything we could get, our legs dangling outwards between the front and hind wheels. This was the provision for three able-bodied men, two, of course, sitting on the driver's perch; but we were consoled by the thought that this was merely a temporary arrangement, as we were to catch the team sent on in a day or so, and would have more room : under this expectation, we laid in the smallest possible quantity of supplies, as the advanced guard carried everything.

Thus, we proceeded to the ferry steamer, which brought us into Kánsas on the opposite side of the Missouri. Here our troubles began ! The smaller pair of ponies of good reputation led the way ; but, unfortunately, the land rose rather abruptly, and much traffic had loosened the sand, so the wheels of the chariot drove very heavily indeed : at last we stuck, and had it not been for the extraordinary stoutness of the last bought pair, who dragged both loads at each recurring difficulty, our waggons might be now in Kansas, as unfortunately we had no tackling for yoking all four to each waggon at hills and other difficulties. The first few miles was through forest, with clearings every here and there, and then we emerged into more open grass-land, with woods all round, till we came to the little village of Wathena ; not remarkable for anything but the euphony of its name, which it shares with nearly all those of similar (Indian) derivation. Here we heard tales of murders, which made me long to get beyond such an Aceldama

as the Missouri and Kansas borders have been for
years.

Having made seven painful miles, and come near
a farm-house, we unyoked, and erected our tent:
a wall tent, so-called because it is more like a house
than the round or " Sibley " tent as it is called here,
and only requires the support of three sticks, two
placed upright and one horizontally. The tent was,
of course, assigned to the ladies of the party; the
men had to sleep " al fresco," or if they preferred
it under the waggon. Milk was procured from the
neighbouring farm, and with the aid of some crackers
did for supper.

26th.—Some of our party had brought a large stock
of bedding. I had not; trusting to our teamster's
declaration that he had an ample supply of blankets,
&c.; so that I found that the damp of the ground
below, and the " inclementia cœli " above, whatever
that might be, would have to be endured with very
little protection. This was, at any rate, conducive to
early rising, and this morning we were astir before
either sun or larks: if there were such birds on this
part of the continent. The ladies got a little law for
their toilets, while we took down the inevitable stove,
tied to the back of our waggon, and found dry wood
to light it withal.

The stove is quite an American's institution, unknown or scarcely known to us ; it does his cooking,
warming, baking, and is the one indispensable piece
of furniture in a house of moderate means ; ours
was very light, had an oven for our bread, and a
place to fry, and a place to boil in.

Now begin preparations for breakfast, which may be
taken as a sample of most meals ; first, then, quant.
suff. of flour is taken out and duly compounded with
soda and cream of tartar to make rolls for the party,
which they term " biscuit "—a great misnomer, as
they never are done enough I think; then quant.
suff. of either ham or bacon is sliced off and fried :
the latter goes by the name of " Billy Russell," on
the plains. Coffee is browned first, then ground,
then made—the true art of having good coffee.
Eggs and milk may be added, but they form no
staple. Voilà le déjeûner ! Dinner at twelve is
generally a biscuit (roll), a bit of fried pig in some
shape, and a glass of cold water with anything
your private fancy may suggest as a " stick." And
supper, breakfast repeated, with hot rolls and butter,
and in addition such small condiments as dried
peaches, apples, or blackberries, stewed with some
rice, all of which I thought extremely good.

Breakfast over, bedding has to be packed, tent taken

down, horses fed and harnessed; so we consider it
reasonably good time if we can be under weigh by a
few minutes after six. Here we come to fresh grief
again; one of our crack little team won't face a small
hill. This time we have to temporize, as a heavily-
laden waggon is easily upset on a hill; but soon our
"vetturino" got a chance at the little delinquent,
and the position of master and servant once well
established, there was no more trouble the rest of the
journey. Soon we emerged from the "timber open-
ings," and got a full view of the real rolling green
prairies of which every one has read and heard so
much. And truly it is a grand sight, that vast undulating expanse of green grass, unbroken throughout
the wide horizon, save at distant intervals by a fringe
of trees forming the margin to some creek, or by a
rare farm-house standing out alone in the wild
wilderness of grass. An Englishman will recall the
hills of Surrey, or the wolds of Yorkshire; but neither
gives any idea of this wide sea of verdure with its
clear sky and fresh breezes. I cannot remember my
first impressions of the sea, but I should imagine they
were somewhat similar. For miles, as you travel
along, you don't see the vestige of a stone or even
gravel. The soil is a rich alluvium, and of course very
easily tilled; the farmers here universally allow one

man to forty acres of tillage—a fair estimate to our notions! The road, if you can call a natural highway by such a name, was just like an avenue in a park (where the main track went) minus the gravel and edging; by the sides where it was not so frequented by waggons, it was much like the road to the Grand Stand at Ascot, in a fine summer.

A few miles brought us to the village of Troy, where we arrived simultaneously with the mail, and this latter brought tidings of the capture of Vicksburg. Talking with some of the agricultural pundits who clustered round the post-office, I ventured with great temerity to think the news was not true. Instantly I saw my mistake—What? doubt the triumph of the cause of right, and that when announced in black and white! Our "boss" told me after we had left the village that I had incurred much suspicion by my unguarded remark; that I was looked upon as "tinctured," and that the consequences might have been serious, had he not poured oil on their outraged passions by informing them I was a foreigner, and, of course, ergo, incapable of forming a right judgment of things in this country.

As we went along, an extremely gentlemanlike old man standing at the door of his log hut offered us some milk, which we gladly accepted; but I regret

3

to say one of the party rather inconsiderately threw
away the surplus on the black ground before the
cottage, where it would probably be noticed, and
might wound the old man's feelings.   True, the man
might have said, like the Calabrian pressing pears on
his guest,—

Hæc porcis hodie comedenda relinquis ;

but the manner of his making the offer was extremely
pleasant and courteous, and are we not told that the
gift of a cup of cold water has its merit?   I forgot
to mention that the little village of Troy, whose
houses you might count on one hand, had still its
printing-office and its paper.   In the evening we saw
a good number of prairie chickens, or grouse of this
country, and am ashamed to say, sacrificed some for
supper.   They were generally wild.   It is strange
that these birds should leave the wild plains for the
neighbourhood of settlements where they can get corn
—" panem et circenses "—in preference to liberty and
a poor larder.

In the evening we camped near a farm-house,
the well being, I think, the inducement : I know I
got a tub of ice-cold water from it at night.   Every
sort of crop and vegetable seems to thrive in this
part of Kansas : I noticed even fields of sweet potatoes.   Isn't it strange that this root when trans-

planted north, should in a year or so turn into the common potato? This looks as if it were the original of our great European staple.

27th.—Rose very early with a view of getting chickens for the pot, but found them far too wild. I suppose Shelley never saw the "sanguine sun rise with his meteor eyes" on the prairie, save in spirit, after the manner of poets; but his description is very life-like. I confess myself to have had Charles Lamb's constitutional aversion to early rising, and to have left such pleasures to larks and housemaids, and therefore know very little of the sun's phenomena at that hour; so in my ignorance I was surprised that the orb of day should present an elliptical instead of a rotund appearance: like the pictures of cherubs blowing a trumpet frantically, his cheeks seemed unnaturally distended. I suppose the solution is as simple as may be, but I " don't see it."

At about one o'clock we made the village of Kennekuk—a little larger than Troy—and going on a little further, came to a shady glen, where we dined on dried beef and pickles, having first. written and posted any letters we wanted at the village post-office. I may remark that I saw stone cropping out here, for the first time on the prairie.

The farms here are almost invariably of one size, namely, 160 acres, that being the number which each man is allowed by law to buy, or to settle, without buying, by a five years' residence. The object of these laws was to prevent land speculators rushing in and absorbing whole tracts, to the detriment of poorer men; but like most sumptuary laws, they break down in operation, and a simple deed of mortgage evades their provisions.

A few miles further we enter upon what are called the "Kickapoo reservations," or land allotted by government to this tribe. The lines have fallen to them, I must say, in pleasant places, as timber, the great desideratum of the prairies, is rife on their lands; and their farms seemed very good, and well fenced. We camped for the night in Grasshopper Creek, or rather, in the wood by it, where we found the mosquitoes very attentive, and a wild cat seemed to be challenging any of the party to "whip" ever so small a part of his weight in a single one.

28th.—Morning chilly and raw, but I think these sensations arose more from want of sufficient blankets than anything else. Reached little Nemaho by dinner time. This is an extremely pretty creek, very well wooded. Oak seems to be the great timber of this continent, and the varieties seem almost endless. There is the live oak of Florida and Texas, said to be the best in the world for ship-building—the ' red oak, the black oak, the white oak, and water oak.

We passed one or two very nice-looking farms to-day, and the owners seemed to think well of their prospects this year. Wheat was in the ear, and seemed not to want much more than a fortnight for ripening. Potatoes, we were told, were a good crop if they got rain enough. Driving along to-day we saw several porphyry rocks cropping out, and the land seemed to contain a larger admixture of sand. Towards evening we came up with a large government team of twenty-five waggons, each having five yoke of oxen to it, bound for Salt Lake City. Our twenty-seventh mile brought us to Seneca, a very neat little village on the Great Nemaho, and here we camped, having only secured one chicken for supper.

29th.—The night was damp, and the dew in the morning was heavy enough to remind one of Virgil's exquisite description of the Mantuan vales, where—

Quantum carpent armenta diei,
Exigua tantum gelidus ros nocte reponet.

The village of Ashpoint we make by about 9·30, and we strike the Little Vermilion stream by dinner time. There was a ranche here, but the lady occupant, on our asking for milk, informed us " her cow did not come home o' nights." There is a station here of the overland stage line, and I had a bit of a talk with the driver, who was a pleasant fellow enough; he had to look after his team of four horses, and drive his twelve miles into the bargain, and for this he received twenty dollars per month with board. He assured me that the facilities for what they call " jumping the pole," or picking up waifs and strays of passengers on their own account were extremely limited here, as one can well conceive: in fact they did not find him in whiskey money. At Salt Lake he told me the drivers drove longer distances, or rather repeated the same distance over oftener, but did not have to look after the nags; they were paid at the rate of fifty dollars a month, with board—no bad allowance in hard times.

This overland mail is a wonderful institution, and I doubt whether, even in Russia, it can be paralleled. It originated in 1860, replacing the " pony express," which was just set on foot to save the great delay of sending letters from the eastern states and Europe to California *viâ* the Isthmus. The time now occupied by this line in crossing the entire continent is from seventeen to eighteen days during eight months of the year, and

twenty-one or twenty-two during the remaining four.
By taking a " through ticket " from end to end you
are entitled to the privilege of stopping a reasonable
time at the intermediate stations ; thus the tedium
of this long route can be much relieved, and some
pleasant excursions, in quest either of large game or
scenery, can be undertaken. The charge for the entire
distance is 150 dollars, and fair meals—for which
there is ample time, not apportioned on the Crewe and
Swindon principle—are obtained at prices varying
from 50 to 75 cents, or 2s. to 3s. of our money ; but
the allowance of luggage is miserably small, only
25 lbs., beyond which a charge of, I think, 40 cents
a pound, is made. This is barely compatible with
cleanliness, certainly not with comfort.

The coach is a large " convaniency," holding from
six to nine passengers inside and one outside on
the box. It is longer than our mails, but not so
high ; it is hung on leather springs, and pitches on
the hills like a ship. The luggage is, strange to say,
all fastened on to a sort of stage behind, covered by
an apron. There is no guard to protect either mails
or treasure ; but then every passenger is expected to
carry arms here. This line from Atcheson to Salt
Lake is owned and horsed by a single proprietor,
and I must say some teams of his mules could not

be surpassed for quality and condition. The Government pays the line a subsidy of a million dollars per annum.

As we were walking along, our driver was attracted by the rattle of a snake; on killing it, we found it was nine years old, as it had nine joints to its rattle. As every one has not seen this appendage, I may state that it is firmly fastened on to the tail by ligatures, though it pulls out without any great effort when the reptile is dead. Each joint looks something like a pearl, or rather two small pearls joined together; as, besides each joint being perfectly distinct, there is a division running lengthways from the first joint to the last; each joint is just a size larger than the one below it, so the rattle tapers down to a very fine point. In each cell there appears to be a kind of hard secretion, which is set in motion by the tail, and this, striking against the thin bone of the joint, produces a noise which faintly imitates a child's rattle, but which is very distinctly heard when close —or stay, I think a better idea will be conveyed by shaking the dry pod of a pea near your ear. Travellers do not seem in great alarm at this snake, as, if you see it, you can always avoid it, or kill it; nor do I think it would ever attack, unless alarmed or in self-defence.

The specific for its bite that seems to obtain most credit is an enormous dose of whiskey,—in fact, as much as the stomach of the patient will bear; on the other hand, I once met a man on whose veracity I think I may rely, who assured me he cured a bite by the simple pig remedy of a mud bath, and after that a long soak in spring-water. "Apropos de cochons," it is said the hog is a sworn foe to all snakes, and eats them greedily; and I have heard in Michigan of pigs turned into swamps actually fattening on the "Missa Sauga" snake, which is accounted fully as deadly as the rattlesnake. I must here put in Herodotus' saving clause, "but this I have never myself seen."

By the evening we made Big Vermilion, a creek beautifully wooded, and with an undergrowth of gooseberries, strawberries and wild grape vines which to English eyes seems astonishing. Indeed, the vine seems quite as much at home in America as it is in any portion of Europe, though I cannot say I have yet tasted any wine on this continent which I much fancied; the "Catawba," which is so much vaunted, seemed to me rough and harsh, and I could not help thinking the California specimens which I tasted mawkish. Though it be a very heretical opinion, I must confess that a glass of wild grape wine which I purchased for a few cents in a country district of Missouri, seemed to me far better than any of the high-priced liquors. But then wine-making is in its infancy here, and when they have had as much practice in this branch of art as they have had at cider, no doubt they will succeed as well.

30th.—An early start brought us past the Vermilions and Smith Station. Near this, I first met that very singular little animal, which goes by the name of the "gopher." It is something between a weasel and a prairie dog, but smaller than either, and with a beautifully spotted skin like a panther's; it runs very swiftly through the prairie grass, in which it has holes, and looks at you in the most knowing way when once under the shadow of its own roof-tree: these holes are, however, not deep, and you can catch master gopher by flooding them. I shall not easily forget the sharp bite I received from one, while trying not to hurt it by holding it as one would a rat or ferret, by the skin of the neck; the little brute had a coil of muscles in his spine which I envied, and could make nothing of whatever. If the wolf be a sad thing for the fold, in Virgil's * estimation, the gopher is equally so to the corn-field; as I

* Triste lupus stabulis.

am told that when the young maize is just sprouting, he will root up a whole row to get the tender esculent to pleasure his dainty maw, so that the gopher may fairly take rank with the *curculio* and other pests which " invade " the husbandman.

Passing along, we saw a very pretty duel fought in the air between the " king-priest," a bird something like the well-known mocking bird, and a largeish hawk, in which the latter was discomfited and fled away. We constantly meet the " whiporwill," so called from the noise he makes ; it is a small hawk which seems to me almost identical with what was called in the West Indies the mosquito hawk. By noon there was some change in the soil and the scenery ; the prairie grew less rolling and more hummocky, and the water-courses seemed to form deeper indentations in the sandy soil ; ledges of limestone appeared in the higher hummocks, and there was more of a mineral character, I thought, in the appearance of nature : on the road I picked up a bit of ironstone which was very heavy.

Soon we reached Maryville, when our eyes were greeted with real stone houses, and some of them rather neatly built ; indeed the village was very neat, and there seemed one or two very fair stores : of course, there was the usual saloon, with its bar

and billiard-room. The thermometer here indicated
82 in the shade. Land about here can be generally bought for about two dollars an acre, if not
fenced or otherwise improved. I was told the homestead law, which provides that a residence of five
years entitles the citizen to his farm of 160 acres,
had been suspended till after the war, as the volunteers
had to get their grants first. These grants of land
were, however, generally sold for a mere song ; as
was the case in the Mexican war.

Passing through Maryville, we came to the Big
Blue, a very respectable river, which we forded, and
dined under the shadow of the trees near it.
Before dinner I took a plunge into the stream, and
thought the moment propitious for doing a little
washing; but alas! while it was bleaching, during
dinner, the linen disappeared, and I can only suppose that a California team which camped by us,
is the better for my loss. Thence we drove to Cotton
Wood, some twelve miles, and camped; making
twenty-seven miles this day.

31st.—Set out walking to-day, and hardly got into
the waggon till we reached Rock Spring, at about
6 P.M., twenty-two miles distant. The soil seemed
much poorer, the sand predominating, and consequently we had more dust. On the road I met a very

large spider, shaped something like the tarantula, and looking like a large hairy gooseberry crawling along. This I found was occasioned by its having a multitude of its young endorsed upon it. The plains here appeared covered with what I think is wild serastrium, whose pale French grey colour I like so much in a garden. The number of waggons here seemed to increase greatly, looking, with their white covers, for all the world like convoys of ships crowding into port; specially when seen climbing up a slope at some distance.

June 1st.—A slight shower of rain lays the dust very pleasantly, and makes the going better. By noon we make the Big Sandy, a well wooded stream, and a ranche being handy, we paid it a visit, and found the lady of the house very communicative. Hearing we came from Missouri, she seemed astonished we had escaped the tax levied upon emigrants from that state, namely, thirty dollars a man, and one cent per pound on all the goods you carry with you. This vexatious imposition is levied, I believe, with a view of hitting those who set off westwards to escape the coming draft or conscription.

Here we met a man who had lost five head of horse kind, and was going to the Otto and Pawnee Indians, camped near Maryville, to endeavour to get some tidings of them. We were rather amused to hear the stories of the *sassiness* of the Indians, since the outbreak of the war; of their throwing themselves in their red blankets on the road, and scaring the oxen-teams out of their wits, and such like tales.

The country to-day appeared poorer—stone cropped out in places, and the gullies were deeper; however, the plains were enamelled with a beautiful kind of wild flox, of the richest ruby colour, and the prairie rose, a sort of dwarf dog rose, was wasting its sweetness in all directions. It seems so strange that we meet no bees or wasps as we move along;—having heard so much of " bee-lines " and wild honey, one is prepared to see any amount of them in the prairie. We make Little Sandy River by about 4 P.M., and camp close to its woody sides. Rabbits seem to abound here; so, in spite of the season, we kill a number for supper, and find them very good indeed.

In this part of the prairies, cotton wood is almost the only timber of any size to be met with. It is a species of poplar, and derives its name from its seed, which contains a sort of fluffy stuff something like cotton. In this respect it is like its namesake in the West Indies, which attains such gigantic proportions, and forms such a prominent object in many of the most lovely landscapes of that lovely land. It is an extremely soft bad wood, but growing as it does to a good size, it suits the purposes of the ranchemen, who do not aim much at stability or permanence in their erections.

In building their log-ranches they do not attempt to saw this timber, and sometimes barely square it with the axe; morticing the logs together in a very rough way, and filling in the interstices with dirt, rarely whitewashed. A large square is then enclosed with a stockade of the same timber, which is called a corrall; a stable is erected in the same rough and ready fashion as the house, and then the establishment is complete. For discomfort and untidiness it would be hard to parallel them even in the neglected portions of the Emerald Island; but then a house in this climate is almost— save for shade and occasional shelter—*le superflu*, not *le nécessaire*; and the absence of mud is a very broad distinction in favour of the former.

It must not be supposed that these ranches imply farming on any scale whatever; they are simply business stations to meet the wants of the emigrants and travellers westward, and therefore each mainly consists of one room, which serves for store, grog-shop, and bed-room by night. In the smaller ones, and they are far the most numerous, the stock in hand may be set down as consisting of much pork and ham, a few pounds of coffee, salt, pepper, vinegar, pearl-ash, soda, flour, butter, eggs, corn, dried apples, peaches in tins, and oysters also, with a Falstaffian proportion of a vile compound of whiskey and I know not what, which is popularly known as " bust head," or " forty rod," because the unfortunate imbiber is seriously affected in either brain or legs, or even in both, before he has gone that distance.

Winter is the harvest for these ranches, for then they have to feed the passing stock on corn and hay, which they retail at the most enormous prices: corn, for instance, which, in the Western States, was selling last year at 20 cents a bushel, is retailed here at two and three dollars, while for hay they ask two, three, and even five cents per lb. But one of their great sources of wealth lay in "trading" oxen. For this purpose they begin with a few of their own, and when a man passes with a foot-sore ox which can go no further, they sell the traveller a fresh one at their own rate, while a dollar or two is considered the " rule of the road " for the jaded ox: or rather was, for competition is beginning to mar this golden age. Under these circumstances it will not be surprising that these rancheros make their "pile" pretty quickly.

2nd.—The night was positively cold and the dew was very scant, so starting early, we made Thompson's Station, where we found a well sunk to the depth of 105 feet. To dig a well is about the first thing a man has to do here, and I must say the people are very civil in allowing every passer-by to use their wells most freely. After this, we passed over a large section of perfectly flat prairie, covered with weeds, among which I noticed, for the first time, Scotland's emblem; it looks, however, a very harmless plant here, and might, I think, be provoked with great impunity. There were also quantities of mimosæ, and though they looked exactly like the sensitive mimosa, these had not the shrinking peculiarity. The Little Blue, a very pretty stream, fringed with a thick growth of cotton-trees, oak, scrub, walnut, and sumach, now lay before us for some distance, and on its banks we camped.

3rd.—Started in good time and made Jessie Ewing's ranche by an early hour. Here we saw a young antelope which had been recently caught, and which was a great pet. We also bought some buffalo meat from some hunters, who had met a great number on the Republican Fork; these men were

4

very anxious about some of their companions who had been carried away too far by the excitement, and had not been heard of for a good many hours. If men and horses behave only tolerably well and prudently, there is very little danger in buffalo-hunting, but when men and horses are new to the work there is some risk in getting carried away by the herd, and so crushed to death. There is also some danger of starvation if you get beyond your bearings in the prairie, with nothing to guide you but the sun by day, and the stars by night. The great amusement at this season of the year consists in catching the calves, by throwing the larriette or lasso over them.

The scenery to-day was lovely, the Little Blue, with its belt of timber, being always in sight; and by dinner-time we struck it again, and found the buffalo steaks admirable, though deficient in fat. Shortly after dinner, as two or three of the passengers were trying to scramble into our den in the waggon, my foot caught in some larriette ropes which were hanging by the side, and before I could extricate it the hind wheel was right over it at the ancle. On taking off my boot I discovered that no bone was broken, thank God, though the bruise was, as they say here, " some considerable." By the evening we struck the Little Blue again and camped; it was a wet and stormy night, and having to sit in the waggon all night, with my foot cocked up, I experienced that ἀταλαιπωρία τῆς ἀγρυπνίας, the wretchedness of sleeplessness which the historian tells us was one of the worst features in the Plague of Athens. At dinner-time we had caught some chub and a funny little fish, called the "horndace," from sundry little horny excrescences growing out of its head, which we found excellent.

4th.—In the morning we had the satisfaction of discovering that our ponies, which were only larrietted together (that is to say, one rope passed round each of their necks), and not picketed, as they should have been in such a night, had strayed; nor did we recover them till 10 o'clock A.M. The roads were, strange to say, perfectly dry, after the rain, and we made Elm Creek by dinner-time; the creek was, however, as they phrase it here, "played out"—as we might say, "used up." Some of the grass on the prairie to-day looked to me precisely like the African "guinea-grass," which grows so luxuriantly in the West Indies, and especially in Jamaica. I also discovered some which corresponded to the "Bahama," which is so affected

4—2

in the latter island for the dressed ground near houses.

Passing a newly-made grave, only marked by a slight tumulus of earth, we made "Thirty-two mile Creek," and camped.

5th.—Finding my leg inflamed, I devised a sort of sling, by hanging a shot-belt from one of the awning supports, which answered fairly. Passing by the bluffs of the Platte, we met a quantity of prairie dogs, which our passengers vainly attempted to shoot, as they never would show more than a few inches above their holes; the number of waggons, and no doubt the fact of serving often as targets, has made these little animals very wary.

I do not know if the prairie dog has been ever acclimated in Europe yet, or is to be found in our menageries; but I should not think it were difficult to do so, as there is always more or less cold weather on these plains; and I should think they would be very useful in banishing rats. In appearance they are very like the guinea-pig, only infinitely livelier and more active, and their colour varies from a very light to a darkish shade of brown, apparently with age. In places where they are bolder it is most amusing to watch their gambols, and it is really very interesting to observe an old paterfamilias stand at the door of his château and bark angrily at you, his tail beating time in the most energetic style to each bark; the sound of which is something like the call of a guinea hen, or rather between that and a maternal turkey calling her brood. Owls, dogs, and rattlesnakes, are said to keep house together; I can answer for having seen the two former constantly together, but I have only met one or two rattlesnakes near the dog towns.

At dinner we heard of a battle between the Sioux and Pawnees, in which the latter had the best of it; indeed, the latter are very hard to beat, for to their native craft, they have superadded the practice of scientific warfare, and understand all about "rifle-pits," and are famous marksmen : as an American volunteer, who knew them well, said, "If we fight the Pawnees it is man to man, and our main advantage would be the revolver, which they do not yet possess."

By the evening we struck a branch of the Platte (about as wide as the Thames at Henley), at a place called Sobiski, or Junction, from the fact of the converging roads from St. Joe, Nebraska, and Omaha meeting at this point. Here we camped.

6th.—In the morning we found, on comparing

notes, that most of us might have said, like Clarence after his first night in the Tower,—

Oh, I have passed a miserable night!

as most bore visible tokens of the activity and zeal of the mosquitoes. As we drove on, we met large herds of cattle bound for Denver, or California. After a few miles we reached Fort Kearney, which is, however, only a barrack for a small number of soldiers; the parade-ground looked pretty neat, with a few field-pieces about, but the stables, as we passed, looked filthy and unkempt. It is a pity that, as a rule, the Americans are too " go-a-head " a nation to insist upon scrupulous neatness in all their public buildings and institutions. I recollect having the same idea forced upon me at West Point, which, as a show-place and lovely in point of situation, ought to be more *soigné*, methinks. Here we saw the wooden spire of a tiny church—the first I had seen for days. The Government are strict in preventing travellers from camping within two miles of the Fort, to preserve the forage for the cavalry horses. Here, too, we meet the telegraph to California for the first time.

Two miles further brings us to Kearney City, popularly known as Dobee Town, a miserable collection of adobed houses; which, however, did a good business with the travellers, and I believe a frontage in Dobee Town commands a good number of dollars. An Irishman from Kanturk, whom I encountered there, informed me a miserable-looking store of this mud fabrication was good for 2,000 dollars. I certainly should be glad to leave the present incumbent "master of the situation." My sole purchase was a sheet of vile note-paper, for which I paid three cents—its weight I should think in silver, if not gold. Wood, we learnt, was so dear that twelve and fourteen dollars are paid for a cord of green cotton-wood.

A short drive brought us to the Platte, which is here a mile and a half wide, but shallow, and full of islands; all efforts to navigate it, even in the shallowest of boats, have proved abortive hitherto. By the evening we made a ranche at Seventeen Mile Point, and camped in a storm of rain, thunder, and lightning, which was so near that there seemed scarce any interval between the flash and the clap of thunder. I passed rather a wretched night in the waggon and got chilled; the rest found a shelter in a house.

7th.—Our ponies had again strayed, and we did not recover them till nine o'clock. From this time our way lay right along the valley of the Platte and on

the southern side, the horizon being bounded by a
line of low sandy bluffs. The road here was very
swampy after the rain of last night, and strewn on
both sides were the "reliquiæ" of innumerable
animals that had been killed, or had succumbed on
this long road, so that we only managed to paddle
through seventeen miles; we then camped between
two ranches, kept by a Frenchman and an Englishman respectively. I found many of the ox and other
teams make a point of reposing on the Sunday—
some no doubt from a wish to observe the commandment, but most, I think, because they feel its practical
benefit, and are thus enabled in the long run to make
better time than the Sunday travellers.

8th.—After a wet night we find the ponies again
"conspicuous by their absence," and did not recover
them for some time. The ranches here begin to show
signs of the proximity of Indians, by their buffalo
robes and peltry for sale. The Cheyenne Indians
are, we learn, reckoned the best tanners of buffalo
robes; an art in which the Indians maintain a monopoly of superiority—the only true kind. Here, too,
we met with a Mormon predicator mounted on a
mule; but he did not long remain mounted, as
on a difference of opinion arising, the moke gave
the polygamist a cropper: thus "spreading the truth,"

as some one aptly remarked—and the only way to
spread such truth as his.

Crossing a bend of Plum Creek, we found three
feet of water running fast in a place which had been
dry two hours previously. However, we contrived
by fastening all four ponies somehow to each waggon,
to get over safely ; but we had rather a squeak for it.
By four o'clock, after travelling roads of the consistency of Welsh rarebit, and tiring the ponies considerably, we made. Pat Mullalley's ranche, where
there were a number of waggons assembled : the
horses all secured by picketing or hobbling, for
fear of Indians, whose lodges were near. Here we
camped, and more rain fell. However, it ceased
towards night, and with the aid of a roaring fire and
a mighty brew of " egg nogg " we contrived to be
pretty comfortable.

I forgot to mention, the day we were at Plum
Creek, that the paymaster of the troops passed by ;
not that that was a singular circumstance, but the
method of his progress struck me as characteristic
of the country. First came the paymaster, in an
ambulance drawn by four mules, and at a short
distance his orderly, I presume. I think this pair
refreshed and went on. After an interval, four
troopers came galloping up anyhow to the ranche,

the paymaster being a long way in advance; but were they going to pass the ranche without a visit? Forbid it the genius of true freedom! so they pulled up deliberately. How much "bust-head" they consumed in the ranche I cannot say, not seeing it, neither can I say when they caught up the paymaster; but I could not help thinking it was fortunate for Uncle Sam that the Indians did not set any great value on either Mr. Lincoln's or Mr. Chase's portrait in the shape of a "greenback."

9th.—This morning proved very fine after the rain. Thinking the hog a very sensible animal and a good plain doctor, I imitated him by giving my leg a long mud-bath, and I think with good effect. As we went on, one of our party shot a blue-winged teal, a bird unknown to us, I think. The tameness of the ducks here was, I must say, shocking to me.

Plunging through mud-holes, sedge, and slush (the Platte valley wants draining sadly in places), we came to Miller's ranche, where we dined. This house, like most about here, bore as its emblem a pair of stag or elk's horns fastened over the door; I could not help thinking what a fertile theme for jests and quips this would have been to any of the wits in Shakspeare's day. At this ranche I was amused by an Iowa lad, who was nominally working at a bit of a trench which a labourer in England would probably have got through in a couple of hours at furthest. The lad told me he was to receive 25 dollars per month from the ranchero, with board, and that the job he was at was the toughest he saw before him; after that he " guessed " there was nothing to do, save a little cooking morning and evening, and " coralling " the cows. His wages were to.be raised if he would stay for the hay harvest. In Iowa he averaged from 30 cents to 50 cents per diem, save in harvest, when wages were better.

By seven we made Dan Smith's ranche and camp. Here we saw an Indian grave, which I thought very curious. It was not more than a hundred yards from the road, and consisted of a hurdle placed on four uprights, about eight feet high; on this the body, sewed up in a linen cloth, was laid, and there it seems it was left. We passed several others afterwards, only varying in the material enclosing the corpse; generally, I think, it was a red blanket. I could not see that any suitable provision was made for these Indians hunting in the future they anticipate, as there was no sign of bow, spear, or rifle. When a chief dies, they say his effects are interred with him, and his war-horse slain, to carry him well in those elysian hunting-fields. As a rule, we were told the Sioux preferred taking their dead with them, and burying them in their cemetery at Ashpoint, some distance up the Platte; where, I was informed, some very strange scenes are enacted. Some of their dead are buried upright, with the faces appearing.

10*th*.—This morning was very fine, though cold; at least, it bore promise of a fine warm day, which was fully realized. By ten we make Gillman's ranche, where there is a large stable and corrall. Cedar here supplants the cotton-wood, as it is found in plenty in the Canons, or ravines between the bluffs. As we burnt it at night, I could not help recalling Virgil's

Urit odoratum nocturna in lumina cedrum.

Soon after this we passed a lot of Indians on the march. Their equipage was amusing: first a lot of skins or robes are tied round the pony; then to these a number of long sticks, which I think must be their tent-poles, are fastened, so as to leave free room for the action of the ponies' hind legs; across these poles a sort of shield or hurdle is strapped, and on this the " papooses " or babies, and occasionally a squaw, sit in state. Thence to Joe Bower's ranche—then McDonald's, at Cotton-wood Springs—and by the evening we make Cotton-wood post-office, where we camp; and, the night looking dubious, we gladly secure a corner in the stable.

The Platte valley about here was so level that all the cricketers of the world could have played without interfering with each other. From the appearance of the line of sand-bluffs flanking the stream on either side, I concluded that the whole of this valley had at one time been more or less the river's bed, till at length the present channel—a very broad one—was adopted.

11*th.*—The morning being fine, and my ancle decidedly better, I hobbled on in advance of our party; not knowing that they would have to go to the bluffs to cut cedar, to last for fuel for several days, there being no wood on our route for miles after leaving this place. After reaching a ranche some four or five miles distant, where a Frenchwoman informed me she had seen nothing of our waggons, I got alarmed at the position, as I heard there was another track by which they might have slipped by; so, weary as I was, I was forced to push on at the best pace for a cripple, and shoeless on one foot.

I had not gone far before I met two athletic-looking Indians, riding unusually fine-spirited ponies. I saluted them with the usual "how," or "how d'ye do?" and received my "how" in return. By this time they had got me between their ponies, and gave me to understand that they wanted tobacco. I had none, and showed them my coat-pockets empty. Then one of them seeing a gold ring on my finger wanted to grab it, but this I would not allow, though I had not even a stick in my hand; then my coat which I carried on my arm caught their fancy; but I would not let them pull it away. I kept backing, and they pushing against me, till at last one signified to me that he would have my ring, and was proceeding to draw his bow in a menacing manner. I laughed, and affected not to understand him; and so, after much pantomime, I was suffered to go: and, let me confess it, felt released from considerable alarm, for a party of soldiers had just been sent to overawe these Indians, who were incensed with the Government for not being paid in gold, according to treaty, but paper; and there were 3,000 of them encamped close by.

At last, thoroughly weary, I reached Jack Morrow's capital ranche, and found the waggons had not yet come up. As usual in the better ranches, there was a good supply of ice here. While waiting for our party in the great room of the ranche, I could not help feeling intensely amused at the manners and customs of the labourers at these establishments. A man would go out—they were doing some building work—for some twenty or thirty minutes, then he would come to the bar, take a "smile" of whiskey, followed by a gulp of water (the usual style.of mixing grog in America), then he would cast his eye over a paper, and resume his labours; and so on, *da capo.*

The "prickly pear" begins to be seen pretty freely in this neighbourhood. It is said to be very good when cooked properly, but I imagine it is something after the fashion of the "limestone" broth in Lover's amusing anecdote.

After dinner, for which we had antelope venison, extremely good, we made Spring ranche, and camped by "Fremont's slue;" "slue" meaning, in Western parlance, a small pond or dyke, generally rather shallow. It occurred to me that in this region of rattlesnakes we who slept "sub Jove" might find them in unpleasant proximity some morning, but the old hands assured us a buffalo robe was a charm against them. Certain it is, no accidents do occur in this way, and every one almost uses a robe in camping on the ground.

12th.—The morning was cool, and we got under weigh by 6.45 A.M. Here I began to feel the effects of those wet nights in the waggon, in a pain in my side, which was ominously like a little touch of pleurisy. However, proceed we must, and the fineness of the climate gave me confidence. Near Bob Williams' ranche we found the flora enriched by multitudes of sun-flowers, smaller than ours, however. Here, too, were a number of Indian lodges, generally beautifully made of white skin: often the summer buffalo's, when the coat is shed. One of the squaws was decked in a Paisley shawl!

Quæ regio in terris nostri non plena laboris !

Passing by Baker's very neat ranche, and D'Orsay Station, we camped by the Platte, having made about twenty-five miles. The fashion of the wells here, which are shallower, reminds me of the old style of Bible pictures. An upright, across which works, on a pivot, a long pole, with the bucket tied on to it; thus forming a powerful leverage by which water is very easily raised. Another feature in some of these ranches, is the stocks in which the patient ox is slung for shoeing, with the leg tied " *a la* Rarey;" for without shoes, soft and stoneless as the roads are, the ox is apt to get foot-sore, specially in winter: but it is an expensive process here, as eight shoes are required for the double hoof.

13*th*.—At dawn we saw some " silver-footed antelope," at which I took a four-hundred yard shot, not being able to stalk them; but, apparently, hit nothing. The sand here was very trying to the eyes, and those who had prudently armed themselves with "goggles" here donned them, and found their advantage. Camping by the Platte we had the advantage of a delicious bathe in its rapid current.

14th.—In the morning we could see no trace of dew whatever, which was a great contrast to Kansas. By the way, I forgot to record that we had now been some days in the territory of Nebraska. It was curious of a still morning to listen to the sound of the bells, carried by at least one animal in each of the herds which were toiling westwards. The bell used is rather a large oblong shape of copper, and makes a much pleasanter sound than the pert tinkle of our sheep-bells. It seems to have a curious effect upon all animals, from the tiny bee upwards.

From Fort Kearney we had travelled generally in a line with the California Telegraph, whose cedar poles every now and then seemed fined down to a dangerous degree by belated travellers short of wood. Our party, who were eminently loyal, attributed this to "secesh"—a convenient cat now a days; but I could not help observing that if mischief to Uncle Sam's property was intended, the wires would have suffered.

Passing "Lone Tree" and "Diamond Spring,"

we come to " Star Ranche " or " California Crossing," where was an excellent store belonging to
a Mr. Beauvais, a man who has accumulated a large
fortune in the Indian trade. The ranche was kept
by a half-caste young man of pleasant manners and
appearance, who gave us a little music. I think I
heard that Mr. Beauvais, like many of the trappers
and rancheros here, had wandered down from the
neighbourhood of Montreal. Prices here ranged very
high. Corn was 2 dolls. 80 cents per bushel, and
sugar, from 12 cents at St. Joe, had mounted up
to 40 cents. Passing " Buck Eye " ranche, we killed
a rattlesnake of considerable antiquity, and camped
again by the Platte, which here abounded in islands
full of osiers. These islands are peopled by beaver
and otter, which in winter are trapped at good profit;
skins here somehow being actually dearer than in
the States. Badger, too, are pretty numerous hereabouts, and I was assured made good pork.

15th.—Our route lay this morning through a
sandy desert, the bottoms alone near the Platte
showing any verdure. We met a very large herd
of cattle of all sizes coming to the El Dorado from
the distant fields of Iowa. Here one of our most
staid ponies got a sudden fright, and our driver
tumbling by the pole had a narrow escape, but

actually wasn't hurt. Walking on in advance, I knocked a rattlesnake on the head, and took eight rattles from him: on this occasion, the rattles alone warned me of his proximity.

At Julesburg, the road branches off to California, and we here bid good-by to the telegraph. Here I met a man who gave me a most wonderful account of the Reece river silver mines in Nevada. He said, he considered he had made his fortune in a single year, and was sending for his family. Leaving Julesburg, we passed over a series of sandy bluffs, very straining for the ponies. Attempts have been made to patch these sand spots with loam from the bottoms, as in rain an amalgam is thus formed. Walking on, we met a rattlesnake, and chased him into a hole, out of which I pulled him, and threw him in the air; which enraged him so much that he bit himself to death: he had not got his rattles yet, a distinction between these reptiles and babies. Passing "Ackley's ranche," a better mud-house, we camped. I took the opportunity of walking across the Platte, which here is from a quarter to half a mile in width, and rapid in parts; it gives the idea, with its shifting currents and sand-spots, of a tide receding from a broad strand.

16th.—So dry is the air that some clothes I left

to dry late last night, are all but fit to wear this morning. It is a comfort, if one is "afflicted in the feet" in these plains, that there is no "gamin" to torment you with an inquiry for "your poor feet." The valley widens here as we move along, and the bluffs on the south side of the river assume an appearance reminding me of the Wicklow hills on the Kildare side of Dublin; the north side, which is not so much travelled over, seems rich in grass. More sandy bluffs had to be passed, and, as we got to the top of one, there was a very pretty view of the Platte, which extended into a basin and was studded with green islets, quite as pretty, I thought, in their small way, as the "thousand islands" in the St. Lawrence, which I never quite appreciated.

Passing the toll-gate, or rather portcullis—made of a pole which is raised for free passage by paying a dollar and a half for each waggon going, and half a dollar returning—we came, without further adventure than killing a watersnake mottled beautifully like a panther, to Spring Hill Station, which bore evidence of the saw-mills near Denver. We then camped at Lillian Springs, where the heaven was illuminated with lightning more fantastic than any fireworks; but there was no rain. At this ranche I felt convinced, by a fence I saw, that an Englishman or Irishman had been at work, so I went in, and found it tenanted by a North of Ireland man; he had left a good farm in Illinois on account of the war, which he disapproved of, and, as he considered talking a thirsty process, he insisted on my joining him in some whiskey, modified by a cordial much approved of, I believe, called the "Good Samaritan." I had my fears as to the results, but they proved groundless.

17th.—Some of our party last night heard "the wolf's long howl on *Colorado's* shore," to parody Campbell's line. In this trip we have only met the prairie wolf, a mean, skulking-looking thing, without the pace or dash of the fox, though like it; but the grey wolf is quite "another guess sort of crittur:" large and lank he is, capable of great mischief; but the enormous number of dead cattle along the road, keep him too well fed to be dangerous. A ranche man told me he poisoned with strychnine thirty-nine one night, besides foxes: the latter are very small, and would, I'm sure, give a very poor account of themselves in a five-minute scurry with any scratch pack of fox-hounds.

Soon after starting we met a lot of waggons from Missouri, and a very large herd of cattle, among which were some nice-looking Durhams. The "boss" of

the team (man, not ox) told us he had been caught a
few days back in a severe hailstorm, and lost three
cows, some of the best, too, by lightning. I ad-
mired the "sang froid" with which he recounted
his losses, saying he was only too thankful he had
escaped so well himself. He had a very fine Here-
ford ox, foot-sore, about which he was anxious, as
he said it weighed some 1,500 lbs. It is surprising
how well some of these herds look, considering they
travel twenty miles a day on an average. Cows
seem very cheap in this part of the country; good
ones only selling at twenty-five dollars, or five
pounds. Some of the people in his party had
caught a very large "cat-fish," baiting with a frog,
while we only bagged small fry, fishing with meat,
or a grasshopper.

Storms on these plains are not uncommon even
in May, and are extremely violent; in winter numbers of cattle succumb under their violence, when
hay and shelter cannot be found for a long distance. It is not long since one eminent firm lost
nearly three hundred in this way. "Denison's
ranche" we made by 9 A.M., then toiling over more
sand, where wild sage and wormwood was the sole
vegetation, passed "Valley Station," and camped
some three miles beyond it. We killed a jack

rabbit, or prairie hare, *en route*, but could not use him, as his long ears had been assailed by nasty parasites—" collecta sorde dolentes."

18*th*.—In the morning I hobbled on over some more arid plains to Moore and Kelly's ranche; there we learnt by a Denver paper that the thermometer there indicates 105; and I hardly think it can be less here. This state of things leads one to appre-ciate Isaiah's beautiful simile of the shadow of a Great Rock in a weary land.

There were several Indian lodges here, and we got the men to shoot at a mark with their bows and arrows; their practice was not wonderful, and I think Mr. Ford would have made them open their eyes rather wide. The bows, which were small, were made like the ancient Oriental pattern, curving in towards the centre, and consisted of a piece of hickory beautifully wrapped round with buffalo fibre, so as almost to look like a solid piece of timber. One of the lads was handsome, and might have sat for a study of an Italian organ-boy. Nearly all the Indians have faultless teeth, a great contrast to their white supplanters. It is said that many of the F. F. V.'s, as the Yankees call the aristocracy of Virginia (first families of Virginia), have a cross of Indian blood in their veins; and for antiquity, what can beat it, save the Hebrew, to which it is said to be cognate ?

Passing Beaver Creek, we camped about 7 P.M. I find the emigration has made pasture on the banks of the Platte very scarce, reminding one of the rivers drunk up by Darius' army: "Epotaque flumina Medo prandente."

Our camping ground and its vicinity was covered with alkali, which is extremely common in these latitudes, and gives names to places. "Some like soda," as one of the party observed.

19th.—The morning was cool, and we got an unusually early start; my ancle felt stronger, and my side much the better for this dry clear air, which gives an inexpressible feeling of lightness and buoyancy. Bathing in a creek by the way, I got passed by the waggons (which, like time and tide, wait for no man), and had to walk nine miles before I could catch them—far too much for my lame ancle. At dinner-time I stalked a fine herd of antelope, but lost my shot through good-naturedly waiting for a passenger. There was a great deal of mirage on the plains to-day—a sort of smoky haze, from which the Smoky Fork river is called. In some lights it looks like a lake in the far distance. Proceeding to Junction Station, so called from the uniting of the North and South Forks of the Platte, the sand looked so heavy that we concluded to camp.

20*th.*—Our fires were lit before 4 A.M., and we were under weigh by 5.35, crossing more sandy and arid plains, till we came to Bijou Creek; a dry watercourse now, but evidencing its being occasionally a home for water, by the poplars which grew in numbers about it. A young bull-dog had followed us from Junction, and it was amusing to watch him hunting an antelope; the antelope, in turn, chasing him back to the waggons when he was quite exhausted, but still keeping out of range. Leaving this creek and the ranche, which was a composite building between a " doby " and a stockade in the Grecian style, we came to a deserted ranche, where we got some wood. We camped soon after in the plain, with scant prospect of fodder for our ponies, save the corn we carried. I should have stated that we had left the line of the Platte at Junction, and were going to Denver by a short cut, known as the " Cut Off," because saving fifteen miles; but it is not popular, owing to bad pasturage.

21*st.*—There being no water for our cuisine, we started at 4 A.M., and made Living Springs, a tidy ranche of pine and shingle, by about 9 o'clock;

meeting any amount of game of all sorts, quite tame, on the road. Had they an instinct of Sunday? At any rate I refused, point blank, to fire at them, as I think created things should be exempted from every species of persecution from man on this day.

Soon after we got a grand view of the Rocky Sierra, partially capped with snow, with Pike's Peak and Long's Peak on either side, standing like sentinels keeping an everlasting watch. They did not tower so far over their surrounding brethren as I expected, considering they are among the high points of the world; but I suppose we were nearly a hundred miles, if not more, from either.

At Living Springs a labourer seeing me reading a novel or book of some kind, begged me to trade with him, and I utterly confounded him, by making him a present of my "travelling library." The Americans are wonderful devourers of reading of all sorts; and their high standard of general intelligence and education enables them to obtain a fair insight into any subject, and to talk well about it. I have often been surprised by the language of men in most subordinate positions, well chosen, terse, and expressive; and it is this general diffusion of knowledge which appears to me so incompatible with the low standard of the press generally, compared with our own! But then

ours is, I think we must confess, exclusively written
for what we should style the intelligent class; theirs
for the mass, which devours the daily papers with an
avidity I never saw equalled: and truly they cannot
be said to be "too pure and good for human nature's
daily food."

The quantity of dead cows strewed along the
road was amazing; and if phosphate of bone become
popular, these plains can supply any demand. After
breakfast, one of our hind wheels got into a rut, and
the tire being lose, it nearly turned inside out. No
smithy was within miles, but most fortunately two of
our passengers had commanded whalers, and were
rich in expedients; so we put in false spokes, and
lashed a cross piece athwart the wheel, till, I
believe, it was firmer than its fellow. Passing
Kiowa ranche, a two-story building, we came to
Box Alder ranche, and camped : the night was
very cold indeed.

22nd.—We were under weigh by 4.20 A.M., and
came to "Cold Creek," shooting a prairie dog
by the way, as here we found them very bold
indeed; then we got to the toll-gate, on the
portcullis plan, and here we breakfasted : and for
as much as the next stage was to bring us to
Denver, the ladies of our party made themselves

very smart, and emerged soon in very different "form" from their chrysalis travelling state.

I would gladly have said a few words about the party who formed "our crowd," did not space oppose it; but one of our lady travellers was so interesting, and made herself so agreeable, and came out, moreover, under such romantic circumstances, that I must say one word about her. Born in New York State, her family settled in Texas, and her lover migrated to Denver, to practise law there; which it appears he did very successfully. To wed him she undertook this long pilgrimage. Fortunately there was no hitch, as her "legal friend" drove up near this place, and took her in his carriage home; and next day they were man and wife : so easily is the knot tied here.

At the toll-gate we found three prairie dogs in a kind of cage in the form of a house, with a revolving cylinder of zinc, attached to it; they seemed rather a happy family, and eat corn.

A few more miles over rolling arid prairies brought us once more in sight of the wooded fringe of the Platte, and in a short time, lo! Denver disclosed itself, nestling in a snug corner of the Platte valley, which is here narrow enough, and separated from the great mountain wall by a plain of about twelve miles. With its bright new paint, and new brick buildings, the town looked very picturesque, and I was much impressed by the smartness of the inhabitants; for we received numerous invitations from "touters" mounted on horseback, to patronize their different establishments. The "necropolis" of this town lies to the left as you enter, and is very neatly kept.

A few minutes more deposited me at the Tremont House, a capital hotel, where I was fortunate enough to secure a bed and room to myself; as I discovered by the evening, when "shakes-down" anywhere were the order of the night. In the younger days of Denver, before hotels had attained even their present development, a bed was deemed quite a luxury; men generally brought a robe and blanket with them, and only wanted a spot to place them in. Now, after nearly a week's experience, I can testify to the great comfort of this establishment, and to its excellent cuisine. It is true, that it is conducted on the most republican principles of social equality; the only qualifications required for admission to its hospitalities being Caucasian descent, for I do not think the President of Hayti himself—the greatest man of the proscribed race I can at this moment recall—would be admitted to its fellow-

ship, and sufficient luggage to make the proprietor
tolerably safe for a few days.   But this, after all, it
shares in common with most *tables d'hôte*, whether
on land or sea.

It was rather an amusing study to observe the different classes who here assemble.   Conspicuous by
their uniforms are the Colorado volunteer officers,
who, in some numbers, seem to live in this house;
then bankers and gold-dust brokers, speculators
from the east, mechanics about to engage in operations in the mining districts, merchants and their
clerks, tradespeople, and every now and then some
" rough and tumble " looking miners, who have
come down hither to spend a little money and see
the world: and, I must say, all classes behave with
a decorum and self-respect, which, in England, we
should hardly expect to find universal.   Indeed,
having heard much of the primitive manners and
customs of the far West, it is disappointing to find
merely a variation of the civilized world located here.
One feels inclined to think that, now-a-days, what
Byron said of a small privileged class, is true of a
far larger one,—

> Society is now one polish'd horde
> Form'd of two mighty tribes, the bores and bor'd.

As far as Denver is concerned, this arises from the

fact of every man in the territory having been an
" advena," not born in it ; for this territory of
Colorado is still, if we count by years, in its very
babyhood — but a Hercules in swaddling-clothes ;
and to pursue the analogy, it has already strangled
the serpents which menaced its cradle, in the shape
of the Indians, whose domain it was ; and who now
beg, where a few years ago, they were lords paramount. The very county in which this young city of
Denver has raised its head is called " Arapahoe
Co," from the Indian nation of that name, which,
however, is generally diminutived into " Rapahoe."

I do not think that one Englishman in a thousand
is aware of the existence of this vast tract of land ;
which, from present appearances, bids fair to become,
in a very few years, one of the richest jewels in
the crown of whatever dominion shall then claim
its allegiance and fealty. Nor, should he search
for it in any old map, will he be able to find its
" local habitation," or even name ; for the latter it
only assumed three years since. " Colorado ! " he
will be sure to associate it with the " Colorados
Claros," of which—if a man of good taste—he will
have such a lively appreciation ; and may probably
conceive it to be a near neighbour to that glorious
valley which blesses the world with its Cabanas,

Napoleones, Regalias, &c. It is but a few short years since geographers described it as the great American desert — a Sahara, " domibus negata," and about twenty since Kit Carson and the present General Fremont explored some portions of it; with a view, not to settlement, but to establish a communication between the eastern and western portions of the United States.

Yet in this town, which numbers some five thousand inhabitants, and where you can get Wilkie Collins's last romantic puzzle, meringues à la crême, and see the Colleen Bawn rescued from her abyss of blue tarlatan, you might four years ago have counted the shanties on your five fingers, and, probably, bought them for a very few dollars. Indeed, it was not till the year 1859, that Denver assumed anything at all resembling the proportions of a town, and only last year the best part of it was burnt down ; but it has already risen from its ashes in renewed splendour, and the civic authorities are reversing the old revolutionary cry of " Guerre aux châteaux, paix aux chaumières," for they are arresting the progress of wooden buildings and shanties, and insist that Denver rich shall dwell in brick or stone mansions.

Carriage across the plains being so expensive,

every effort is naturally made to make the place as independent and self-supporting as possible, and nature has assisted this endeavour to a great extent, by furnishing in the neighbourhood almost everything necessary for civilized man. Thus, furnaces are being established for smelting the iron ore, which is found in large quantities and very pure; coal is procured close to the surface without any labour; and though the land cannot yet compete with California or Salt Lake in its yield of cereals, its capacities are very superior to most of the eastern states, and to European soil generally, even in this respect; while for raising vegetables, it is, perhaps, unequalled; potatoes, cabbages, and beets attaining proportions here, which I am almost afraid to record, for fear of being suspected of exaggeration. Mindful of the old Joe Miller, of the huge cabbage and huge iron pot, I will be silent about that plant, but will content myself by saying, that the yield of potatoes may be averaged at two hundred bushels per acre, without any manuring and scarcely any tillage, while single tubers of several pounds weight are not uncommon. Indeed, here and in Kansas, I was continually reminded of Douglas Jerrold's *bon mot* about Australian soil—" tickle it with a hoe, and it laughs with a harvest."

6

The average of Indian corn has been about forty bushels per acre; wheat has been generally about that standard, and oats above it, while beans and peas give a very good return. However, farming is in its first stage as yet, and the requirements of the peculiar soil and climate are scarcely studied: certainly, as yet, they are by no means understood. For the history of farming here is simply this:—at first, every new comer hies to the mines, and prospects for claims, if an early arrival; if a late one, either buys one or assists in working an already developed " lead." As he is rarely even a small capitalist, his resources begin to fail; in most cases the yield of his " gulch diggings " or " quartz mining " does not support him; his only resource then is to " prospect " for a likely ranche, and as numberless streams pour down from the Rocky Mountains, he selects a spot, builds a log-house and fences as much of the 160 acres custom allows him as he thinks he can till: and so he works on; but nearly always with the intention of resuming mining operations so soon as he can raise sufficient capital, either by continuing cultivation or selling his " claim " to some later adventurer than himself.

But it is as a stock-raising country that this district merits most consideration. Poor as the grasses

look, and sandy as the plains show, representing—
save in the bottom lands close by the creeks or
streams running from the mountains—all the shades
of brown paper, they contain the most marvellous
fattening properties for all sorts of cattle and horses;
the distances performed by the latter when merely
fed on this grass and the condition they keep
is almost incredible; while cattle turned out poor
in autumn become fat by spring, and manage to get
on very well, even in snowy weather, without any hay.
Sheep have hardly been introduced in sufficient
numbers to justify any conclusion being drawn about
the profits to be derived from them as an article of
commerce; but, looking at the high price wool is
likely to command for some time, and to the enormous profit derived from sheep-farms in New Mexico,
which is very similarly circumstanced to Colorado,
I have no doubt that a flock of sheep, if properly
watched and duly protected from wolves, by "coralling" at night, would yield a farmer a fortune in a
very few years.

Owing to a slight remaining weakness in my
bruised leg, I have not been able, as yet, to visit the
mining districts, or penetrate far into the mountains.
One excursion, however, in which I carried a rod and
line and baited with the grasshoppers I found on

my path, fully repaid me for the climbing and toil
it entailed, not only by a basket of very fine trout
caught with great ease, but by the infinite variety
of scenery which it afforded to the view. On one
side of the sierra there were grassy slopes and beautiful woody glades, while the other side resembled the
wildest scenes in Dalecarlia, which the last Exhibition
has so familiarized to us; every now and then,
by the margin of the mountain torrent, one had to
struggle through masses of wild hops, seringas,
clematis, vines, hazels, gooseberries, wild-currants,
and cherry-bushes; with mahonias, and a few ferns
a little higher up the side, and quantities of lupines,
hair-bells, and China primroses. Then the fragrance of the pine-wood is the most subtilely deli-
cate I know, and would, I am convinced, become
infinitely more popular than Frangipanni or wild
violets, could Messrs. Piesse et Lubin only catch
its fragrance as it flies; and as they have generally
succeeded in arresting the volatile essences and giving
them for use to the community, I commend this task
to them.

Though I have not yet visited the gold mines, I
have been to some pains to obtain reliable informa-
tion with regard to their yield, or the expectations of
it. Hitherto it may be said that the adventurers who

came out during the last five years have done every thing one sees in the shape of improvement; and, as they brought out barely any capital, it follows that the civilization before one is derived from the gold yield: in addition, it is estimated that twenty millions of dollars, prior to this year, have been sent on to the States during that period—no small yield, considering the quartz-mills have only been lately introduced, and that the methods of extracting the precious metal are still very imperfect. However, now that capital is slowly beginning to pour in, there is no doubt that great results may be anticipated during the next five years; for it is admitted that, cord for cord— a measure of 128 cubic feet, generally applied to wood measurement—the quartz in Colorado is far richer than in California: and I believe the quality of the gold is also considered superior. To show the unsatisfactory nature of the processes used for extracting the precious metals hitherto, I may mention that some recent experiments on a new principle made on "the tailings" have shown them to be capable of yielding much more than the original ore.

The high price of labour—which varies from five and six to two and a half dollars per diem—militates of course greatly against the full development of the mining capabilities of this auriferous region; but though the wages be high, there is no scarcity of "hands." The attractions of the gold-fields, combined with the wish to escape " anywhere, anywhere " from a fratricidal war, have caused an enormous "stampede " of working men from the Western States especially; and, though this number has been much thinned by corresponding movements to even remoter gold-fields in Washington and Oregon, there is still a large supply available : though, as usual, the employers, looking to the high wages they have to give, consider it far below their wants and wishes. Tradesmen here can generally average from four to six dollars a day, and assistants, who in England would hardly aspire to earning anything, can often command as much as two and three dollars a day, with board. A gunsmith, with whom I had some conversation, assured me he would be too glad to give English lads, who had been accustomed to work at his trade, as much as three dollars a day with board and lodgings; and I may mention that the lads who wait at table in this hotel get from thirty to forty dollars per month, while the cook— who finds, however, his two assistant boys—gets as much as 150 dollars per month.

From what I had always heard of the "rowdy proclivities " of dwellers in gold regions, I expected that Denver would have proved no exception, considering its origin and its remoteness from the *soi-disant* regions of civilization; but I confess that since my arrival—though that period embraces the great American carnival, the 4th of July—I have seen nothing approaching to turbulence or disturbance of any kind: indeed, I have not seen a drunken man yet, which is saying a great deal for a country where "smiling" is the general rule, and where the means of intoxication are so ready and so cheap; in fine, I think the famous despatch may be parodied into "Order reigns in Denver City." In the earlier days of the town, no doubt, there were many scenes of violence and homicide enacted, and horse-stealing, the great crime of the West, was very rife; but when the evil became intolerable, "vigilance committees" arose, and dealt so sternly and summarily with the criminals, that the slower process of law is now amply sufficient for the requirements of society, and vindicates the majesty of justice whenever such majesty is supposed to be outraged.

Like all mining countries, where fortune is made a goddess and given a place in the hierarchy of the sky, gambling goes on to a most unlimited extent, and counts its votaries by the hundreds.

The worship, it is true, is not conducted in very stately temples, nor are the hierophants very distinguished for gifts and graces; but then, like the "portal of black Dis" ("nocte dieque patet atri janua Ditis"), fortune is accessible at all hours of day and night to "noble sportsmen," and may be wooed at monte, faro, rouge et noir, and a game which resembles "blind hookey," but which is known here as "blind buck." The only meretricious or adventitious excitements I ever saw in the *salons de jeu,* were a couple of musicians, on a daïs at the extreme end, playing to very inattentive ears. I have been told that the "upper ten"—for an aristocracy forms even here—eschew these popular resorts, and worship with closed doors; but to their esoteric mysteries I have not yet been admitted.

I have little doubt that when the Pacific Railway, already begun, has brought the Rocky Mountains within the limits, or nearly so, of a long vacation tour, Denver and its *entourage* will become so essentially a part of the grand tour which tradition and fashion have combined to render obligatory on the Englishman, that I must not omit a few words about climate, which is so essential a condition not only to life, but especially to travellers' life.

When I first arrived, I was greatly struck by the

different appearances of the faces here from the eastern visages I had just left. There, ·dyspepsia or the effects of fever and ague, or consumption, were too plainly written to be ignored by any passer-by, on a very large per-centage of the population; here I see nothing but health visible, and with it that enjoyment of every-day humdrum life which is, probably, as infallible a sign as any other of the " mens sana in corpore sano "—which, perhaps, we prize so highly on account of its rarity.

During this month the heat is, no doubt, excessive, the thermometer standing sometimes as high as 100 in the shade; but still it is a very bearable heat, and the nights and mornings are delicious. The winters are extremely short and pleasant; a fall of ten or twelve days snow, during which the sun is generally warm at mid-day, constituting the cold sea-·son. Then, in the height of summer the "tierra caliente" can be exchanged in a few hours for the pleasanter regions of the " tierra templada," or even for the snows and frost of the Range which towers continually over its lower tiers of subject hills; and in the entire district the general absence of dampness and rain gives a buoyancy and feeling of zest and exhilaration which is rarely met in European latitudes.

The inducements to travel to these regions are so numerous and varied, that I shall mention a few of them very cursorily. The Doctor Syntax school can here find the beautiful and picturesque in the amplest and wildest profusion; while the lover of the grand and majestic in nature, can here see his wildest dream realized. To the sportsman these mountains offer unlimited resources, and a climate where, during winter and summer, he may "camp out," needing nothing but the skins of wild animals, and, perhaps, a blanket or two for protection; while the range of large game is unequalled, except, perhaps, in Africa and India. There is nearly every variety of the deer tribe, from the elk to the antelope; also mountain sheep, mountain lions, a large species of puma, wolves, bears, and, if he chooses to descend to the plains, buffalo-hunting: which, however, to me has little more attraction than hunting the "calf" in merry England. The fisherman will find the trout in the upper waters of the rivers, which find their sources among these everlasting hills, very large and very accessible, and a large variety of other fish which to him will probably be entirely new; while to the scientific traveller, the flora and the "crust" of the earth will present an endless and ever-interesting study.

I have already spoken of the advantages these regions offer to the farmer and artisan, and will only add, that I believe the small capitalist of a few hundreds, or fewer thousands of pounds, can here find most profitable and comparatively safe investments for his means ; as the resources of the country are being daily developed, and enterprise is unbounded, only waiting for its lever—capital.

I will only add that, should these few lines about a very interesting country, induce any one to follow my traces, I will recommend the " party " (which word is now accepted as signifying many or one) neither to travel by the stage-coach, nor do as I did, but to purchase his own conveyance at any of the outfitting places in Kansas or Missouri ; and in the enhanced value of his teams westwards he will find his expenses almost covered.

CHAPTER II.

Talking of the Alps, the Apennines, the Pyrenean, and the Po.

To persons about to cross the plains, and visit the Colorado portion of the Rocky Mountain slopes, I will volunteer the following advice, drawn from a not very agreeable experience.

Don't fancy that because this is an age of capitals, and because Paris is France, Denver represents the *agrémens*, or gives an adequate idea of the territory of which it is the metropolis—though, "more Americano," not the political capital (well may Yankee politicians as a rule shun the publicity of a large city). And, more especially if the season be that of the summer solstice, avoid making a sojourn there of more than a very few days consecutively; for I verily believe that Sirius has had it under his special guardianship and protection in this year of grace. I can most conscientiously aver, after a tropical experience of several years, that I never was in a human bakery so fiercely heated as this Palmyra of the desert ; and never—no, not even in the sandy streets of Kingston, Jamaica, or the sun-smitten terraces of Montego Bay—knew I heat so pervasive, so almost omnipresent and omnipotent as here. Indeed, I would suggest to some enterprising and more humane Teutons than their brethren in Strasburg, that a colony of northern geese might be developed into " foie gras " on the banks of the Platte far more naturally, argal, far better than by any artificial caloric ; and as miners (the word may also be spelt with an *o*), like sailors, reck little the expense when appetite is in question, I think a bright field for enterprise, hitherto unexplored and untrodden, lies open to the bold caterer to popular gastronomy.

It was my fate to discover, after waiting patiently for letters, that my budget had been mis-sent to some place in Nebraska ; and not wishing to lose them by having them forwarded to some point further west, I determined to abide patiently till the long course of posts—the " Parcæ " of modern life—should bring them to their original destination. In the meantime I managed to pick up an attack of fever and ague, by bathing in the cold waters of the Platte during the heat of the day ; which I was informed (after the evil was done, of course) was the very acmé of imprudence, as all similar ablutions should be either postponed to the Greek kalends (a suggestion intolerable to the bold Briton, whose cleanliness is popularly supposed to move "pari passu" with his devotion), or else be performed at a very early hour of the morning, before the sun has got quite "fixed up" for the day, or Aurora has left the saffron couch of Tithonus.*

And yet, in spite of these stings and arrows of outrageous fortune—or, dropping the Ercle's vein, untoward circumstances—I can't find it in my heart to malign this port and happy haven to many a traveller over the American steppes, and which I hailed with such pleasure after a month's trajet over that vast land-ocean; nor will I shake off the dust of my feet unkindly now that I am in the purer region of the Sierra, and some six or seven thousand feet above it, and upwards of eleven thousand from the sea's level: nay, I will rather accept the plea put in by the inhabitants—who for the most part, architects of their own fortunes, and architects of Denver likewise, are extremely proud of their own creation—that this year is, for heat and drought, exceptional; that the surrounding plains, which now represent in hue the various qualities of sugar to be seen sampled in a broker's office, from the clayed Havanna to the dark

* Tithoni croceum linquens Aurora cubile.

produce of Guiana, are sometimes comparatively green at this season, and clothed with succulent herbage ; and that the oldest inhabitant (of four years' standing) never did experience such heat, and such dust.

Let me rather incline to the belief that I visited Denver at the most unfavourable time, when the prairie-flower was not in her best looks or most agreeable temper—(there is a city, too, on the banks of the Thames, generally voted unsavoury in August) —for cities and flowers are, as our neighbours, *d'outre manche*, say, "journaliers ; " and sure " even in the loveliest climes light breezes will ruffle the flowers sometimes." Indeed I am quite ready to credit, what every expert declares, that the winters and late autumns are here unrivalled—" world-beaters," as a friend of mine said the other day : for a Yankee thinks it a small thing to beat a neighbour or a rival; and as, according to his creed, America in 1812 boldly went to war with France and England, and challenged the world, " non sine gloria," so in comparisons, creation alone will satisfy the circle of his criticism.

" Est ubi plus tepeant hiemes ? " Where, though fires late and . early are welcomed, an overcoat is a superfluity as a rule, and very often a linen ephod is a sufficient protection from the " inclementia cœli." Indeed, spite of detention, my recollections of Denver are pleasant enough in many respects. Though I cannot recall any vision of very fair women, the better part of creation, if sparsely, was not unworthily represented; and at the churches, if the inward adornment was symbolized by the neatness and good taste of the bonnets and dresses, the pastors may well be proud of their polyglot flocks—Dutch, French, Irish, Poles, &c.

Apropos of churches, how is it that in almost every part of America that I have visited, the musical portion of the service is conducted with an amount of good taste and care which I confess I have found much to seek in out-of-the-way places in England, and in corresponding spots in the Emerald Isle is altogether wanting? It cannot be for lack of materials, for I believe that, owing to the general prevalence of lung complaints in America, the voices of a given number of men and women would be found to contain more harmonious quality in the Old Country than here, if speaking be any test. But without pretending to assign a cause for the result, or suggesting that the voluntary system has anything to do with it, I merely state the fact, that in this respect I think our cousins have set us an example worthy of all imitation ; and I may add that in the Episcopal and Catholic churches which I visited in Denver,

I found the magnificent services of both rituals performed in a manner which surprised me, considering the locality, and the fact that the Anglo-Saxon—unlike the Spaniard—is generally supposed to care first for his mill and factory before his thoughts diverge to church extension.

Indeed, I must say that all over the States, so far as my wanderings have led me, I have found almost invariably the greatest attention paid to what may be termed the " sensational element," such as music and floral decoration; which, if condemned by the severe Iconoclastic school, appears to my unsophisticated reason a beautiful dedication of good gifts to the Giver of all blessings: at any rate it has the virtue of withdrawing the attention from the general poverty and meanness of the temples here, in an architectural point of view. I shall not easily forget the glorious and jubilant profusion of violets and camelias which adorned a church in New York that I attended on Easter Sunday, recalling as they did the idea of the Queen's apparel, as sung by the projector of the most glorious temple ever probably raised by piety to the service of the King of Heaven.

While thus digressing on the subject of taste in matters ecclesiastic, I may add that, *me judice*, in

the mammon of unrighteousness also, our cousins
have in some notable respects shot ahead of us. I
allude particularly to shops and their decorations :
not to mention the stores of New York, some of
which, such as Stuart's, Ball and Black's, and
Brooks', names taken *au hasard* as they recur to
me, are for proportion, organization, and internal
decoration unapproached by anything in London ;
though I have no doubt their contents would be easily
surpassed by those of many corresponding houses of
far less pretensions there.   But even in Denver one
or two of the stores, the value of whose stock was
probably intrinsically small, displayed a neatness and
good taste in their arrangements which we might in
vain look for in larger towns in England ; a result to
be attributed, I suppose, to the great French element
in this continent, and to the admiration there exists
for everything French, which has continued a
national sentiment ever since the days of Lafayette
and Rochambeau.

In summing up judicially the case of Travellers
v. Denver, I must not forget one favourable consideration ; namely, its universally diffused prosperity.
I saw there no signs of poverty; and I believe every
man, woman, and child enjoys there all that is
externally necessary for life and happiness, unless

a higher civilization has raised any one above the level of the ordinary sources of gratification: and such a class will probably not be found within its precincts for many a year. This circumstance ought to go far for a favourable verdict among Europeans, at any rate. This general absence of the insignia and livery of poverty and mendicity is certainly very striking to any one who knew Ireland before the famine; nay, to those who have travelled much in that country even recently; and it exists, generally speaking, all over America, so far as I have gone. But the prosperity of this little half-way station to the Pacific (really third-way only), is eminently remarkable.

I have sometimes thought that much of that inordinate spirit of self-laudation and bounce which Europeans so commonly complain of as peculiarly the "type Américaine," may be traced to the want arising from never, or comparatively seldom, having those sobering, humiliating, and yet elevating and purifying feelings which contact and intercourse with poverty and misery will call forth in natures not wholly devoid of sympathy thoroughly exercised. And this remark if true about men, will apply far more to the case of women.

Then, surely in Denver, if anywhere, the dignity of labour is vindicated; for there, in the cool of the

evening, after supper, outside the crack hotel—and a
miracle it is considering " the where "—will .you see
the high dignitaries of state (known by the vulgar
sobriquet of " big bugs ") " from the Governor down
to the clerk, *not* of the Crown, but whatever corre-
sponds to it—and even to the waiter lad who an hour
or two ago ministered to your wants—all sitting
down peaceably together, smoking and chatting without any *embarras* of condescension on one side, or
mauvaise honte on the other, but seemingly, if not
absolutely on a level, yet very nearly so.

A little attempt is made at social distinction by
the volunteer officers off duty ; but the feeling is
generally too strong against it, and no sin is accounted more heinous than that of "putting on
style " by an officer : I should be sorry to be the
captain with such a reputation who led his company
into action !

And yet there is a shibboleth, a test which no art
can evade, and a crucial test that must be endured
before this society, seemingly so radical in its
equality can be entered ; and that test is " race," nay
rather " skin." The sitter must be Caucasian *de
rigueur*, and woe be, even here, to the fairest of Ham's
descendants who should venture rashly to intrude
himself between the wind and their nobility. Thus,

for instance, the cook of the hotel, whose wages are quite equal if not superior to the average of the minor and medium livings in England, would no more dream of sitting down where those waiter lads are nicotising the atmosphere, than he would in the presence of Jeff Davis himself; though he must know full well that the *New York Tribune,* his friend Horace Greeley's organ, has an extensive circulation in Denver, and that some of the inhabitants are afflicted with what is popularly known as " nigger-on the-brainism :" for politics and social science are two different things. The Yankees allow the proposition, but deny the corollary; so the ban remains, strong as ever: and it applies as well to the so-called inferior races, such as the new and old Mexicans of the lower caste (popularly known—at least the former—as " greasers"), a dusky compound of Castilian and Indian blood.

The only prospect I can see for the removal of such a stigma, seems to lie in the power of money; for the nigger out here will doubtless in some cases accumulate wealth in time; and this lever—greater than any ever wielded by Archimedes—will, I think, effect far more than any victory gained by coloured arms, should such a result ever follow from the arming of the sable race now progressing so fast

throughout the North. For, let us not forget, that
in the war for independence, the blacks fought well
and truly for the liberty of their masters; and
American history has not blinked this fact, though
the record of the requital of such service will be a
harder task for the historian to compile !

While telling one's souvenirs of dry dusty Denver,
—a paraphrase of the " dear dirty Dublin " alliteration,
familiar to all who ever sojourned in that city—let
me not forget the military element which enters so
largely into the composition of the body social.
Colorado has, I think, furnished some 3,000 volunteers out of her population, now scant though so
rapidly increasing, of whom a considerable number
are quartered at the newly erected barracks, close
to Denver, called Camp Weld ; the remainder occupy
frontier posts, such as Forts Garland, Laramie,
and Lyons, to overawe the Indians, and afford
a modicum of protection to the settlers moving back-
wards and forwards over these enormous plains.
Though these troops have not taken any part in the
more historic scenes of the rebellion—or civil war,
as I should more properly call it—some of them
have done as " tall " fighting as any in the war
hitherto ; though, for want of proper trumpeters,
their fame, like that of other Agamemnons and

Cromwells guiltless of their country's blood, has been hidden under the ungrateful bushel of oblivion. Be it mine to let in a flame of light for a momentary space!

It seems that, in 1862, the Texan Rangers—of whose fame as marksmen, riders, and frontier men, the European world is not ignorant—took it into their heads to besiege Fort Union, between Denver and Santa Fé, then thinly garrisoned; with a view of securing the arms and munitions of war then so much desiderated by the Confederacy, and also of occupying it as a post of vantage ground, which would give them a key to New Mexico and Colorado, and enable them to cut off the enormous waggon traffic which exists between these places and the Eastern cities. No sooner, however, did the Colorado "boys" hear of this, than they hurried by forced marches to attack the invading force; and after a few sharp skirmishes and a sort of battle at Valverde and Pigeon Ranche,—when for the numbers, I believe, the losses were heavy—they compelled the Texans to make a most disastrous retreat across the mountains, abandoning their waggon trains, and losing a great number of their force in the retreat, from cold and want in the mountain passes. Since then the "Lone Star" State, mindful of this heavy blow and great discouragement, has directed her energies to other quarters, and has amply redeemed at Galveston the laurels lost in this raid.

The Colorado volunteers are very proud of their achievements on this occasion, and boast themselves about the "toughest cusses"* in the Western army; which, in turn, vaunts its superiority, and, I think, not altogether without reason, over the eastern Federal troops : who, however, have recently, when moved west, showed good fighting qualities, when well handled. Witness the last campaign in Tennessee! They are a very rough-looking and undisciplined body, but like Joey B—, are, doubtless, rough and tough, and ready too, and, if well drilled and officered, would, I am sure, be a formidable force to encounter ; but in their present organization they do not look very different from guerillas ("des brigands," as a French traveller I encountered in Nebraska called them), save in a certain uniformity of arms and attire. This, however, has its limits for officers and men : some affect the kepé or French cap, others the sombrero, peculiarly characteristic of western Americans, and which looks in

---

* " Cuss," an eminently American word, answering more or less to our " chap," though a little more prononcé.

many cases as if it had been imported from the regions of private life; only it is adorned by the crossed sabres, the cavalry badge of the United States. They are, I think, the best mounted cavalry I have seen in the Federal service.

I fear I have often broken the tenth commandment in part when looking at some of Uncle Sam's troop-horses; which, though far too light for our notions, combined more blood and bone than is generally seen in America : though but little groomed and attended to (well fed they certainly are), they display wonderful condition,—the result, I think, of the dry climate, which is eminently favourable to the horse, and the extraordinary nutriment contained in the grasses of this country. Certain it is that horses and men both look a thousand times more like service than the caricatures I gazed at with astonishment lately in Washington and Virginia.

The circumstance of these regiments being so well mounted is owing, in a great measure, to the unhappy state of the land. For "suspects," "sympathizers," "copperheads," "dough faces," and such citizens in the border States, feeling that their horse property is extremely insecure, and daily liable to levy, confiscation, and the tender mercies of those who differ from them in their views political, have brought them in numbers out here; and thus a much better class of animal than usual is secured for "the service." Add to this, that a large part of the horses to be seen in these latitudes have been " jay-hawked " at some period, and brought out here for fear of recognition. And it is not to be supposed that the horse-lifters would select inferior stock.

Before leaving Denver, I should not omit to mention that, unlike most towns of its size—indeed, I think in this respect it stands unique—it boasts a Mint and Assay Office. Hitherto this has been the result of private enterprise, which, in America, at any rate, is so far ahead of their Government; but latterly the United States Mint has made some progress—that is to say, a wooden shanty has been selected, over which is hung a portentous sign, telling you (at least by symbols) that the United States will here some day issue their own coin: indeed, a Government official, who will preside over it some day—unless removed, as is more than probable, in the next general election—takes his pleasure in Denver.

The history of this Mint, and the manner in which an appropriation of a great many thousand dollars, to establish this institution, melted away like a snow-wreath, without more visible result than that which

I have stated—save the invisible one of lining the pockets of committees, who sat on it till the great golden egg got fairly addled—is merely one of the numerous examples of the manner in which public money is dissipated in this country. Against this no voice is raised; as in the first place, who among the " wire-pullers " is pure enough to cast the first stone ? and in the next, four years soon revolve, and then—why, the " outs " may expect their " innings."

Apropos of this subject, I shall not easily forget the impression made on my mind when I first visited the continent, by the cool, matter-of-course tone which every one assumed in talking over the sums which the public rumour—so often a libeller and slanderer —said General Butler and members of his family (notably his brother) had made, by means which we should consider simply infamous in any executive officer in our service. " It was only Uncle Sam, and he can afford it ! " " Nunky pays for all ! " " Every one else does the same," might be heard bandied about, or words to that effect, in the various circles ; and few seemed anxious to ascertain if the aspersions were really well-founded, or, if true, to characterize such conduct by its just title of infamy.

Towards the close of July I turned my back on the " opes strepitumque " of Denver—for, fortunately for

the denizens, the pall of smoke so familiar to us as
the drapery of a large town is wanting, though coal is
plentiful in the territory. Taking a few necessaries,
rolled up in a waterproof lashed to the back of my
Mexican saddle, and carrying my rifle and fishing-rod
in my hand, I started with the intention of reaching that night Central City, which lies embosomed
among the peaks of the Sierra in a westerly direction some forty miles off. It was late in the afternoon when I left the Tremont House, and " le pre-
mier pas " wasn't at all of good omen ; for, wishing
to cool my horse's legs, I passed the wooden bridge
and rode him into the Platte, which here, though not
deep, is very rapid ; somehow the noble steed got
frightened at the swift current, crossed his forelegs in
trying to turn back to land, and in a minute more I
found myself in the stream, and my gun and rod
somewhere at the bottom. However, I fished them out
somehow, re-mounted, and though the buckskin one
wears here when travelling, galoshed over your shoot-
ing-jacket and trousers, is rather an enemy to water,
I found the drying process much quicker than I could
have anticipated ; so little moisture is there in the
warm surrounding atmosphere. In fact, I was evapo-
rated by the time I had ridden twelve miles.

A few miles' ride brings you to Clear Creek, a

mountain stream which flows down from the Range, and once really deserved its nomenclature ; now it is muddier and more turbid than the Thames at Blackfriars, owing to its extensive use in the mining district. These streams form a sort of oasis every few miles in the arid plains, for on their banks, generally running east and west, settlements and ranches cluster thickly; and irrigation being generally adopted, a wide margin of emerald green, dotted with trees, is seen meandering from the mountain side far as the eye can range, down the plains. Fourteen or fifteen miles brings you to Golden City—a wooden town, raised by speculators, who fancied that because it lay right at the foot of the mountain pass, it would arrest a great portion of the trade going and returning ; but they reckoned after the fashion of Horace's rustic, for the human stream flows on faster and in deeper volume each year, but stays not for them, and consequently it remains comparatively a " Deserted Village," though the political capital of the territory.

A little further on, the hills open into a canon, or pass, called the Golden Gate, through which you must pass to the El Dorado of this country. Here you leave the spurs of the mountains, which slope very gently down to the plains, and you gradually get into the solemn scenery of pines, spruce, and

huge bald rocks, through which the road winds with
such gentle gradient that sometimes you are scarcely
conscious of ascending. Indeed, nothing has struck
me as more wonderful than that, in a continuous
ascent of some 11,000 feet from the Missouri level,
one encounters no worse obstacles in the shape of
hills than one would in an ordinary drive in parts of
Wales and England.; so beautifully has nature laid
down that grandest highway of nations which will
soon unite the Eastern and Western hemispheres
by its iron bands—the great "vinculum" of modern
days, the railway. For who can doubt that when

Hi motus animorum atque hæc certamina tanta

.   .   .   .   .   .   compressa quiescunt,

one of the first works engaged in will be the Pacific
railway?—if, indeed, one railway be deemed sufficient
for the growing and continually expanding wants of
commerce. There seemed a great deal of traffic on
the road, and mule and ox teams were continually
passed; but, in spite of that, numbers of rabbits
kept emerging from the brush, and afforded good
practice for the revolver, which forms part of a
traveller's equipment in these mountains.

There are ranches all along the road, where you
can get entertainment for man and beast, though at
stiff rates; hay being retailed by the pound and corn

likewise : but, considering the difficulties in making
commissariat arrangements, I do not think the charges
exorbitant. For instance, at the "Michigan Ranche,"
some twenty-five or twenty-seven miles from Denver,
I got some supper for self and a feed for my horse
for one dollar ; and fortunately in America there are
no poll-tax arrangements for servants to be paid,
under the penalty of contemptuous looks and a
few sarcastic observations uttered " sotto voce," as
with us.

From this point for a few miles the ride was wild
and eldritch in its character ; no travellers or teams
were met with, and the overhanging pine and spruce
fir intensified the darkness of night, while the fitful
moonbeams revealed strange shapes at intervals
among the boulder rocks and withered pine branches,
reminding one sometimes of Gustave Doré's etchings
of "the wandering Jew." At last lights began to
gleam in the distance, and the noise of the stamps
of the quartz-mills, and the rushing of water in
sluices, broke on the ear. Soon you find yourself
riding through the village of " Black Hawk," which
contains some quartz-mills of good renown, and close
to which are the celebrated " bobtails " and " Gre-
gory " lodes—here invariably termed " leads ;" then,
in another mile, riding through the intermediate

village of "Mountain City," you find yourself in "Central City," the capital of this Western Ophir, where I had no difficulty in finding a berth for my horse, but had to draw two human coverts, in the shape of hotels, blank ere I could get a billet for myself.

I have now been here for some days endeavouring to master the arcana by which—

Effodiuntur opes, irritamenta malorum,

and in exploring the various sources from which the gold is obtained; the result of which I propose to sum up in the following few pages. But first I must premise that I am totally ignorant of the sciences of geology and mineralogy, and, therefore, can only undertake to use the popular and untechnical language for the various objects which came under my observation; preferring this to cramming up a series of technical terms—miner's cant and jargon—and in all probability displaying my own ignorance by their inappropriate use.

The three towns of Black Hawk, Mountain City, and Central are situated on a ravine or "gulch" down which a small mountain rivulet pours, with much noise and brawling; but with, this year at least, a very slender volume of water—the lack of which element militates greatly against all surface mining. Hills rise very abruptly on both sides of this ravine ; once clothed with pine, but now dotted with the stumps of their former tenants, and bearing only a plentiful crop of the artemisia, or wild sage, which is characteristic of the entire western district.

Following the main street in Central, and proceeding further up the hill, you come to the town of Nevada, which almost crowns the mountain, and looks down upon the gulch at some distance below. Taking these towns as a centre, and describing a circle of a little more than half a mile, you embrace the best part of the auriferous region that has as yet been developed; with perhaps the exception of the Russell Gulch, which no doubt contains rich lodes, but which has as yet contributed less than its neighbouring gold-fields to the aggregate of mineral wealth in the territory.

Taking the gulch first, it presents the appearance of a mountain torrent, which has suddenly swelled up and brought with it an enormous collection of stones and débris, depositing them on both sides of its normal bed, into which it has as quickly relapsed, retaining only the complexion of the mountain clays which have defiled its purity. On coming nearer, you will observe a number of sluices placed along its channel, and parties of three or four working

8

at intervals of some hundred feet from each other.
One of the men is standing by the sluice below the
others, throwing away the stones which the water
brings down, with a sort of long fork, or what they
call in Ireland a " grape," while his confrères dig up
the dirt in the neighbourhood of the sluice and throw
it in, stones and all.   This is the whole process of
gulch, or surface mining, which has been very profitable; but it is now admitted to be nearly " played
out "—in other words, the field is nearly exhausted.

Then comes the work of examining the sluices for
the result of your week's operations, and taking out
the coarse gold; which catches in the grooves and in-
equalities of the " riffles "—a sort of rack of thin pine
laths inserted as a species of false bottom in the sluice
—while the finer particles of gold adhere to the quicksilver laid in the sluice to catch them, and which,
when retorted, yields the desired gold.   Thus it will
be seen that this species of mining is a simple operation; and, given a "claim," or *locus standi*, no
further capital is required for embarking in it than a
few simple tools, a few boards, and a small amount
of quicksilver.

However, it has its drawbacks, like everything
else. A claim of 100 feet is easily exhausted; and
though it may contain good paying material, and

a few nuggets (which, however, run very poor and small here), it may prove unequal to the expense of the labour. Add to this that it can only be worked in summer—as both water and mercury get frozen in winter—and that it depends entirely on a good supply of water ; which in a year of drought such as this is retailed by the " Ditch Company " at the rate of 75 cents, or 3*s*., per inch per day. The gulch miners, however, whom I have questioned, seemed satisfied with their labours, and said they were making good wages—which means some five, six, or eight dollars a day : no bad pay, considering that the work is not heavy here, and far healthier than in the shafts ; and hence hands at gulch mining seldom get much more than two dollars a day, while the lode miners get from that amount up to four or five.

This latter species of mining is the speciality—the great industry of the place—and by its success or failure Colorado will rise or fall. But failure seems at present a contingency of the remotest character, and to be dreaded about as much as the conflagration of the Platte, or the evaporation of the Mississippi ; for even last year, with capital of the most limited amount, and very imperfect resources in science and machinery, twenty millions of dollars were, I am assured, extracted from the gold-fields of Colorado : this year, more capital having been injected from the East, and more confidence being generally felt in the prospects, a much larger harvest is confidently anticipated. All round the hills are evidences of lodes in every stage of progression. Looking up from the town, these scratchings catch the eye in every direction, presenting the appearance of a cordon of rifle-pits hastily dug for the defence of the villages : these are lodes which have been discovered, but whose working and development is either abandoned for want of means, or other good cause.

Then, all around, are shafts which are being vigorously worked with various appliances. Some have steam lifting power, others a horse " whim," while others in poorer hands have only the rude construction of wells. As a rule—owing to the fact of the claims being limited to one hundred feet, (though any number of one hundred feet claims may be legally owned by an individual,) and that the owners are generally men of small means—the *modus operandi* has hitherto been the sinking of a perpendicular shaft, and thus following the lode downwards, instead of cutting it by means of lateral " adits " or tunnels : a more expensive method in the first instance, but far more satisfactory in its results, as the water is thus more easily drained off, and the ore more easily conveyed to the surface by tramways from the shaft.

The history of a "lode" (within a few years I mean, for who could hope to guess even at its real history in the long past with any accuracy?) is this :—The gold-seeker goes out "prospecting," and comes to a "crevice," where the "blossom" or burnt quartz rock cropping out, and the appearance of a sort of wall round it, inspires him with strong and justifiable hopes of success ; a little labour with pick and shovel extracts enough of the rock to make an experiment, and if he finds, on pulverizing the stone and detritus, enough promise to warrant his sinking a shaft, his first step is to record his claim ; which he can do by payment of fifty cents, or two shillings, to the recorder of the county or district. He then commences operations on it ; otherwise, were he to leave it unvisited for some time, he would probably find it "jumped :" in other words, seized by some adventurer like himself ; for mining law or custom—now recognized by the tribunals of the country—declare, that if a man does not develope his claim by at least some preliminary digging or improvement, he must give way to some one else who will do so. This admirable regulation was made in early days to prevent monopoly by the greedy, and to give all a chance.*

As a rule it has been found here that lodes which pay near the surface improve with depth; though it does not follow that some which scarcely pay at first, will not pay well further down. But, granting that the lode pays well for some time, at length, in almost every instance, a period comes when the lode disappears from sight; this is called here, "being in cap," or in other words, the "key rock" is reached. And here commences the real struggle between man and gold; for the cap may be very thick, and very tough, and no one knows when it will be penetrated and the lode refound; and during all this time no "pay" is extracted, so that if the proprietor's means are slender, he generally fails; but if he has any capital left after the contest, he gets a new and better start, this obstacle once overcome.

It is rather amusing to hear the conversations on the subject of this *bête noire*. "How are you getting on at Nevada, friend?" "Oh, worse luck, we're all 'in cap' there this week." This seems rather unin-

---

* I believe these early laws have since been modified by the Legislature of Colorado, and mining property put on the same footing as real estate. There are no alienage regulations, and property may be held by the inhabitants of any portion of the globe.

telligible to the uninitiated, but here it tells a
lamentable tale of failures, blighted hopes, and the
last dollar spent in vain ; therefore, naturally, "cap "
is a personage out here.

I am not going to invite you to descend a shaft
with me, either in a bucket or down those very steep
ladders—sometimes made of a single pole with rungs
stuck through it, such as you see in a bear's den
in the Zoological Gardens—as the journey is not
interesting or clean ; and generally the terminus
is extremely narrow, affording room for not more
than three or four men, who are busy blasting away
at the rock, generally too hard for a pick : for here,
following the law of nature which proclaims that—

> Nothing in this world is single ;
> All things by a law divine
> In one another's being mingle—

gold is generally found in chemical or mechanical
combination with iron, copper, silver, and lead, as
well as sulphur; and I believe that if proper appliances were forthcoming, the baser metals would in
many cases pay for the working of the shaft and mill,
and leave the gold net profit.

The rocks being sent up to the top in buckets,
there follows the task of separating the " wall rock "
from the paying material, easily known by the glitter

of the pyrites upon it; then it is carted off in ox-waggons to the crushing-mill to be pulverized, having been first broken into small lumps. Many claims have their own mill attached to them, by which much expense in cartage and crushing, varying from 35 to 75 dollars per cord of 128 cubic feet, is saved to the mine.

These crushing-mills are for the most part worked by steam-power, though a few have luckily secured the more economical agency of water. When in operation they look something like the machines used for driving piles, though on a smaller scale; for a wheel turns a shaft, attached to which are a number of iron crooks, which in turn have a number of long iron drivers or hammers appended to them; these are lowered and raised, and thus crush the stone on an iron die or stamp, inserted in a metal cup: a little water being introduced slowly through a pipe, to facilitate, I suppose, the pulping process, and to carry out the "dust" on to tables of copper or mixed metal, which have been previously coated over with quicksilver. When these tables are cleaned, —as they are by scraping them with a piece of india-rubber,—an amalgam is obtained of gold and quicksilver, which only requires the retort to obtain the grand desideratum.

I should not forget to mention that below these sloping tables are placed certain blankets, through which the water percolates : this is done to catch the gold, which is mixed with such a metal as lead, with which quicksilver will not amalgamate. The sand or dust which remains after the gold has been caught by the quicksilver is not thrown away, but after a time may be again passed through the mill; with such success that some " tailings " have yielded more gold than the original rock—showing how extremely defective was the primary process.

The mining mind is just now full of another method, which promises brilliant results; and though I cannot explain the details, I may state that its object is to desulphurize the quartz, or extract from it, by burning, the sulphur with which it is often so heavily charged.

The first question that naturally suggests itself to the practical mind is, of course, "Do these mines pay ? Have fortunes been realized ? or are these miners merely adding their number to the long train of those who, ever since the days of Cortez and Pizarro, of Gilbert and Raleigh, haunted by the splendid golden vision, have followed the shadow to the neglect of the real substance, which in less brilliant guise lay unused before their eyes ? "

To the two former questions, I think an un-
hesitating affirmative reply can be given, while an
equally unqualified negative awaits the latter inter-
rogatory.

That these mines *do* pay is, I think, evidenced by
the very existence of the territory—of these towns
and buildings which are rising in every direction, and
which are already beginning to discard their primitive
wood, and assume proportions of stone and brick:
" si monumentum quæris, circumspice."

When it is recollected that the class of people who
came here in 1859, and have been arriving ever since,
were, with hardly an exception, poor adventurers
(some so poor that they had to make the passage
across the plains on foot, carrying their little stock of
worldly goods in hand-carts), with few chattels beyond
the waggon and the cattle which conveyed them from
the States, and without " credit " to draw on ; and
that so dear were provisions, and so far beyond their
reach, that a large portion of these bold spirits sup-
ported life, and even realized some small capital, by
the produce of their rifles, and by trapping, which
they followed in the winter, devoting the summer
months to surface mining ; and when, further, it is
recollected that only the hardier and more sanguine
remained, while a large proportion of the fainter-

hearted returned to the States, declaring that the land was no Canaan, but a howling wilderness,—it will, I think, be readily admitted that these mines have been a great success: and this in spite of great obstacles.

For besides the scarcity of capital and the want of labour in the earlier stages, and the discredit thrown upon the opening prospects of these gold-fields by those who went away in disgust, much injury has been done by the "stampedes" caused by the tidings of discoveries in new and still more distant regions. Some of these reports turned out eventually to be the merest "Bogus;" but they had the effect of withdrawing capital and labour from these settlements, and also of unsettling the popular mind for a long time. And, besides, nothing perhaps was more wanted than real mining knowledge; for those who undertook to mine here brought little or no science to bear on a work which requires necessarily a very large amount: hence, as might be imagined, much time, labour, and even gold has been wasted in unnecessary experiments, and in groping painfully after better methods. True, a few old Californians came over, attracted by the ring of the metal; but the country was so different, that their experience—though of course of some value—

did not add so much as might have been expected to the general stock.

Now, however, that the stamp of great success is set on these mines, science will be brought to bear upon them. Already there has been of late a large influx of Cornish miners — the free lances of the profession — who have come from Lake Superior, where they were employed in copper mining; and they may be expected at any rate to improve the practice, if not the theory, of the mining here. And those to whom I have spoken complain much of the rude way in which many of the shafts have been constructed, and the great risk which is consequently run in working them. Indeed, I am sorry to say the percentage of loss of life and accidents here is very great.

To the second query I would answer, that four years is a very short time to realize anything like a fortune, or even a competency, when no capital, or scarcely any, is employed. Yet it is a fact, that though here no rich nuggets have suddenly raised the lucky finder from poverty to comparative affluence, still, fortunes have been made; not colossal it is true, but amounting to a moderate independence. Some have been frittered away at the gambling-table and in other sinks for money which ever abound where gold is found, while others acquired with difficulty are being gradually dissipated in foolish undertakings; but a few have been retained, and are being turned to profitable uses. But I think the fact of any fortunes being thus acquired must appear passing strange, to any one coming from a highly-civilized and over-crowded country, where all the avenues to riches are closed, save to capital and very superior intelligence; for there, undertake what you will, you will find it impossible to succeed, save through the well-worn grooves in which genius is compelled to move.

True it is, that the greater part of the success here must be attributed to good luck; for let a man be ever so good a miner, and ever so prudent in husbanding his resources and putting them to the best advantage, following a lode is sheer venture, and if the " cap " prove stronger than the miner's purse, farewell to hopes of fortune in that direction.

It is often remarked, that taking the entire number at work in mining, it will be found that even a low average of wages has not been realized by all. This may be true in many places, but I think not here. But, even if it were a fact in Colorado, it could be easily accounted for, and brings no discredit on

the mineral wealth of the country. For there is no
doubt two classes of men will, as a rule, succeed
here.

First, miners who can labour steadily, and have
sufficient stamina to work continuously in a lode,
can save from three to five and even six hundred
dollars a year, after paying expenses. This, however, is not given to all men, as besides the accidents
I have alluded to, the work in the shaft is very
trying to some constitutions—partly, perhaps, owing
to the quantity of arsenic found there, and partly
to the great dampness of many—and many men
cannot work more than three weeks in the month,
if so much; not on account of the hardness of the
work—for it is not very straining—but its great
unhealthiness. Such men, if very steady and prudent, will in a few years accumulate a small
independence. For money doubles itself very quickly
here, the rate of interest having been, not long
ago, twenty-five per cent. per month; and that *not*
without security.* But the danger is that, in an
intoxicating atmosphere such as this, they will be
dazzled by the prospect of a rapid fortune to be
made by mining on their own account, and the luxury
of being, in their turn, each a " Bos; " and, of

* Even now 10 dollars per 100 dollars a month is the usual rate.

course, the chances of success in this new line are barely even.

The second class consists of business men who have some idea of mechanics and steam, and who possess a moderate capital of from five to twenty thousand dollars. Such men are almost sure to succeed here; but that is not saying much, as such men would be almost sure of getting on well in any part of the States, with even far smaller means.

There is a capital which many adventurers bring here which is worth more than its commercial estimate, and that is the determination to succeed if enterprise and daring can effect it. The great indifference to failure which is a great characteristic of this country, and which in the case of dealings with others is often pushed too far; but, above all, the great adaptability to any employment which distinguishes most Americans.

We in England, accustomed to the minute subdivision of labour, are very content with excellence in one single branch, looking no farther; the American, however, as a rule, is content with a far lower standard in any one thing, but he ranges over an infinite number. It is quite a common thing to find a man out here who has begun life at home on the farm, then turned sailor (often

whaler) for a few years, perhaps then gone into
some business on his own account, and is now
here a bit of a miner, carpenter, blacksmith, wheel-
wright, or very possibly in charge of a steam-engine.
Their versatility is unbounded ; their confidence
beats Lord John's, as illustrated by Sydney Smith ;
and I sometimes think that some of the features of
Juvenal's Greek apply to the American of this
century—

Medicus, magus : omnia novit.
Græculus esuriens in cœlum, jusseris, ibit.

Many of the men here have failed in the Eastern
states, and had their energies wonderfully quickened
by the process, and by the fixed resolve to redeem
their fortunes ; most of them out here, too, have
evidently been well educated ; as will appear if you
look at the autographs in an hotel book, where every
arrival inscribes his name ; for these contrast very
favourably with a similar number taken, *au hasard,*
in an eastern city.

Of these mountain cities (we should call them by a
far humbler title in Europe) I have hitherto said but
little ; on the principle that the Spanish fleet in the
ballad could not be seen " because 'twas not in
sight :" and really there is but little to say, even of
" Central," the greatest among them all.   Mr. Trol-

lope, the great λογόποιος of the day, said, if I mistake not, that New York contained little or nothing to see. How would he have dismissed these aggregations of log-houses, and shanties, interspersed with a few fair buildings of better stamp? But I think his fastidiousness led him into error about New York, and I am sure that, even in Central, a Dickens would be able to see much, and describe more. My powers of observation, however, being of the most limited scope, I will only make a few general observations on these

Præruptis oppida saxis.

Of their situation, following up the course of a mountain stream, I have already spoken, and I think it would be very picturesque were it not for the bareness of the surrounding mountains, which have been denuded of their shade and ornament; but the views in the neighbourhood are fine, though monotonous. On one side stretch "the plains" eastward; while westward, and "excelsior," is the snowy range, distant but a few miles, while north and south extend endless mountains clothed in the everlasting sombre green of the pine forest. The climate is delicious, perhaps a few degrees too hot for an Englishman's notions during some hours of the day; but the evenings and nights are unsurpassed, and

9

the air is so highly oxygenated, so buoyant, that you really require some acclimatization to walk up the steep paths, without frequent halts to survey the scenery and catch your breath.

Then the atmosphere is so pure that your vision soars far further than in the foggy curtain to which our eyes are too well accustomed, and this extension of the faculty of sight is in itself a positive pleasure!

At " Black Hawk " a very neat little wooden church meets the eye, with its gilt spire at the top—a symbol, I suppose, of the wealth it surveys, part of which has been so well directed. There are various other places of worship in these towns, but, so far as I have seen, they consist merely of the apostolical ὑπερῷα, the lower story being devoted to secular purposes. Strange to say, one sect of Christianity makes this meeting in an upper room, if not absolutely a part of their faith, at least of their practice; and yet it is hardly reasonable to suppose that the early Christians congregated upstairs, save for purposes of secrecy or *faute de mieux*: and after the lapse of Eutyches, I should think the custom would, where practicable, have been abandoned.

I was, I confess, much struck by what I witnessed *àpropos des églises,* on my first arrival in Central. On Friday evening I repaired to the " Montana," or Mountain Theatre, a rough-hewn building of pine —with a parquette and gallery—capable of accommodating a large number. There I saw *Hamlet* performed, and though the ghost was not very spiritual, Gertrude not very queenly, and the courtiers not very courtier-like, yet the play was, on the whole, very well put on the stage; even the Prince of Denmark, if unlike Fechter's impersonation, was, I thought, really very well rendered.

This was one surprise; but the next was far greater, when, on the following Sunday, I was invited to hear the Bishop of the diocese (I think) preach in the same building, and administer the rite of confirmation to the candidates who might present themselves. And so at three o'clock it came to pass that the parson told the sexton, and the sexton tolled the bell outside the theatre, and at half-past the service began—the curtain being raised. There, sitting in the conventional sofa of the stage, was my Lord Bishop, magnificent in his robes, and with him, of course, an assistant priest. A table placed on the stage, close to the footlights, represented the altar; while near the orchestral seats, a harmonium was placed for the choir, who sat round it, and rendered the musical portion of the service— a large one too—extremely well.

I may here observe that the American Episcopal Church have, methinks, shown great good taste in the way they have modified their liturgical service; which is almost identical with ours, except in a few particulars demanded by their different institutions, and by the change of the archaisms into modern phraseology. 'Thus, for instance, in the Lord's prayer, "which" is rendered "who," as more pleasing to modern ears ;. and in the liturgy "wealth" is translated into the more intelligible word "prosperity."

The theatre was, I was glad to see, pretty well filled, and I do not think I ever heard a more temperate and charitable defence of the formulas of the Church—or I should say the Episcopal branch of it established in England and America—than I heard in the sermon preached by Bishop Talbot, from the text, "What mean ye by this service?" Might not this good example be more generally followed in these days, when the want of church room is universally deplored, and the means of erecting new buildings are not immediately forthcoming?

From ecclesiastical heights to gastronomical reflections is a great descent (though I think there is a connection, and no distant one either, between the church and good living, singular and plural), but I must, in taking leave of Central, say a word about its larder.

Whence the fat beeves come from, or how the cattle about here keep in flesh, is a very marvel to me ; for I see no grass, save a blade every now and then : but in this bite there is a magic power of fattening, they say ; and certain 'tis, cattle fatten on these mountains, even in winter, without hay or other food. Then the supply of their splendid salmon trout is very good ; and in the winter and fall, deer, elk, and antelope are very abundant, and a cinnamon bear may be seen sometimes dependent from a butcher's hooks, so that the miner is at least very well fed.

Game was very plentiful all round here a few years ago, and I was assured that mountain lions and wild sheep—the animals described by travellers as jumping down precipices when pursued by wolves or other deadly foes, and alighting safely on their huge horns, which, however, is denied by the hunters of the neighbourhood as Munchausenish—had been seen across the street not so long since ; now, to paraphrase the well-known lines of an Oxford prize poem—

> Scared by busy man from his own hills,
> The lion fled the loud resounding mills.

And a good long distance has to be travelled over ere the feræ of the mountains may be encountered.

As for the ladies of Central and its entourage—pardon me for introducing them in this remote portion of my jottings, after notice has been taken of so many objects in the animal, vegetable, and mineral kingdoms : the fact is, I considered the subject too serious for my notes, and intended to have passed them with only the silent homage a true man ever accords them in his heart, though pen and voice may not be loud or eloquent. Yet they are the real ornament of Central; and is it not as a tribute to them that all these jewellery and finery shops are maintained? Is it not owing to their influence that these rough places of the earth have been made to feel the power of refinement and civilization, and that the miner, instead of degenerating into a gnome or troglodyte, becomes a good citizen, imbued with all the charities of life?

This happy state of things has not, I believe, been of very long standing; as, for the first few years, the place was scarcely fit for the presence of women; but now they are pouring in fast from the States: these "diggings," like our Indian possessions, being an admirable market for many who have not succeeded eastwards in drawing prizes. And as they ride along the mountain slopes of an evening "en Amazone," with the most coquettish habits you ever saw, decked with all sorts of pretty little gold (or brass) buttons like an hussar's jacket, you might "disremember," as the Irishman said, very easily that you were on the Rocky Mountains, and might fancy yourself transplanted to the neighbourhood of Innspruck, or some other spot in those mountains of old civilization.

There is another large mining district in this locality, about a hundred miles south, in the vicinity of the South Park, called "Buckskin Joe" district; but though the lodes there promise even fairer returns than those in this neighbourhood, they belong principally to even poorer men than the "claims" hereabouts, and consequently have not been so far developed; but they are well worth a visit, I am told, if only on account of the surpassing loveliness of the scenery about there. Indeed, no traveller should think of leaving this country without visiting the three Parks, which are to be found within a compass of about one hundred and fifty miles, and which form a most peculiar feature of the Rocky Sierra. They are known by the names. of North, Middle, and South, and are huge basins in the heart of the mountains, whence issue some of the large rivers which water this part of the continent; the vegetation in them is abundant, and they are peopled by almost every species of wild animal. Should time permit, I trust to visit them all during the fall months, and, unless the reader be tired of travelling through this country, I will be happy to communicate my experiences of wild mountain life in my next.

CHAPTER III.

On sylvan scenes intent.

THE America of 1863—or rather, to speak according to facts, the Federal possessions on that continent— may be classed under four main categories or divisions, to wit :—Battle-fields, spittle-fields, gold-fields, and game-fields. The nomenclature will no doubt be much cavilled at, but can any one deny that this classification is at once comprehensive and specific ? distinguishing in some notable respects the genera and species of the districts in question : as was required in my juvenile days by that wise pundit, Mr. Aldrich, the Lindley Murray of logic ; unless, indeed, my memory has played me a scurvy trick after her frequent fashion, now that Consul Plancus has given place to the majestic Kaiser of the Tuileries.

Of the battle-fields I had seen enough—far more than enough—in the desolated homesteads and the levelled woodlands of Virginia, lovely and picturesque even amid all the surrounding ruin, and though reeking with the hecatombs of the invaders and the invaded slain on her hundred Aceldamas !

The spittle-fields comprise those "centres of civilization," the eastern and western cities, μητροπόλεις καὶ πορκοπόλεις, where mammon and shoddy are worshipped day and night with a fervour worthy of the · worshippers even of the great Diana of the Ephesians ; and which, save in their being more purely commercial, and in some instances of grander proportions than their European rivals, present but few salient points for notice or comment. As compared with the capitals of Europe, one is reminded of Hood's line about Amsterdam or Rotterdam, I forget which—

A sort of vulgar Venice reminds me where I am.

But while thus daring to sneer my sneer at these vast developments of unparalleled enterprise and energy, in an æsthetic point of view, let me never forget the eclectic few, the âmes d'élite, to be met in some, nay in many of these human hives; but like all nature's treasures, such spirits have to be sought for diligently, and seldom come under the notice of the casual tourist or cursory observer, unless specially favoured.

To some of the gold-fields of the Rocky Mountains situated in Colorado, I have already partially introduced those who have patiently accompanied my wandering steps across the green prairies of Kansas, and the sandy Saharas of Nebraska. It remains then only to give a few glimpses of those great game-fields on which civilization has not yet, *more* Mr. President Lincoln, set her encroaching foot, where the Caucasian race is comparatively unknown, and the Indian still reigns supreme over· the subject creation, in vast παράδεισοι or parks far away in the heart of these Andes of a northern hemisphere.

Three such great natural plateaus lie within com-paratively easy distance of Denver city, and are named respectively, South, Middle, and North Parks, from their relative positions. Of these, the first has lost its charm of wildness from the fact of some rich gulches having been early discovered in its vicinity, and it has thus become settled and already semi-civilized ; but the middle and north were still almost virgin soil, and therefore promised a better harvest.

Having settled "the where," remained the solution of "the how;" perhaps the more difficult portion of the problem, for the outskirts of the middle park are a good two days' journey from Central City, and a snowy range or Sierra Nevada, only to be surmounted in a few places, has to be crossed, ere the Goshen of your anticipations can be reached, or even seen: and once there, you are as completely isolated from everything that man as a shopping or purchasing animal may want, as if you were chained to a rock in mid-ocean like Miss Andromeda, or on a mountain like Mr. Prometheus. True, a company of the brave Colorado volunteers had been sent to a point in the Middle Park to repel an invasion of Indians, or to overawe them, and I had been offered the hospitality of their camp; but this I concluded to be a poor way of exploring a new country, though presenting temptations to a votary of mere comfort—"comfort scorned of Yankees," so often—and I gladly embraced the offer of being allowed to accompany a party of four who were going to hunt and trap professionally, so to speak, and who proposed being absent for a few weeks.

Accordingly a day for our departure was fixed, and having some time to spare, I set out for Empire City, which lies at the foot of the snowy range, and which is the usual portal of the Middle Park; but as we had arranged to go by another pass in a totally different direction from Central, I was anxious to see that portion of the mountains, of which I had heard very favourable reports, both for scenery and minerals.

Riding then in a south-westerly direction, I

passed over the bleak surrounding hills, now shorn of almost every vestige of a tree, and so full of prospecting holes that they looked as if rival armies had been disputing every inch of them, and had been incessantly occupied in throwing up these small earthworks; the streams looked as if some mountain had been suddenly let loose on their beds, and every vestige of soil being swept away, had left them merely an accumulation of stones in great piles—so thoroughly had they been searched by the miner. I then came to a "divide" in the hills, now timbered, and following a canôn, commenced a long descent between sheer walls of rock and timber, very picturesque in spots, which continues for about a mile. As you near the bottom of the canon, indications of mining energy are not wanting, and shoots of pine boards convey the quartz at a fearful rate some hundreds of feet from the lodes on to platforms, from whence it is carted off to the crushing mills.

At last, as you approach the end of the ravine, the lovely valley of Idahoe, or "the gem of the mountains," as the Indians have well named it, breaks upon you with a beauty which man the ravager has been unable to efface, in spite of his wooden shanties erected in the fairest portion of the greensward, and the various appliances for bar-mining which mar the

smooth margin of the stream running through it,
making its crystal lymph as foul as bilge-water: for
here rich "bar-diggings," have been discovered along
the banks of the river, and have in a few instances
paid handsomely this year.   Bar-mining is not
unlike gulch mining, except in being far more
laborious; owing to the size of the boulders, which
in vast numbers the river has brought down in its
freshets, and to the fact that the river water must
be kept continually pumped out of the holes made
by the miners, a process effected by an ingenious
machine called here an "hydraulic."

The only natural curiosity I saw at Idahoe are
some hot "soda springs," which an enterprising
doctor, or an individual so called,—for where the
majority of the folks you meet are "judges" and
"majors," 'twere hard if medicine had not its pro-
fessors and votaries too with honorary titles; after all
as sensible as many of those distinctions granted by
our universities to eminence in spheres as unscientific
and unliterary as can be imagined!—had recently
purchased, and hoped to advertise into a fashionable
resort for the rheumatically afflicted, whose name is,
I fear, legion here, owing to the wet nature of the
mining operations.   Following up the stream, which
now narrows into almost a gorge, now expands into a

rich vale, you come to " Spanish Bars," and soon afterwards to " Empire City ; " a title which must have been given more in the spirit of prophecy than from any existing applicability, for the only sign of a city existed in about a dozen mean log-huts and a few brace of frame houses.

I was told that the town was growing in the direction of some " patch diggins " towards the spurs of the mountains, but my curiosity was not strong enough to induce a visit. Having a day to spare, I put up at a log shanty, which represented the " Clarendon " of the place, and where a modicum of hay in sacking was given you for a shake-down. I fished the stream upwards, above its mining pollutions ; but I confess with indifferent success, the fish being small and shy. Next morning, having paid my bill—which " Boniface " must have made out in the prophetic vein also, as the log-house and single bedroom for many occupants swelled in the bill to palatial dimensions—(would I could have paid it by a similar draft on my expectations !),—I discovered that my horse was dead lame ; so, as Central City was eighteen miles distant, and our start for the parks was imminent, I had no alternative but to " trade " off my halting steed for a sound pony. This I effected without incurring the heavy loss I might have anticipated ;

considering that I was at the mercy of the man with whom I dealt, and that nearly all the western men are brought up, *ab ovo*, in an atmosphere of "horse-trading," and are as much addicted to, and as keen thereat, as the Irish squireen of the West is at his favourite pastime of "knocking"—a process, I need not explain to any one who has ever attended an ordinary at either of the horse-fairs of Banagher or Ballinasloe.

Indeed, I may here say that such horse "copers and chanters" as the western men I never met. Much they certainly *do* know about the noble animal, and much they affect to know which I think lies beyond their ken. For instance, they make no difficulty in telling horses' ages, after that grand climacteric of eight years has been passed! The result of my trade was a very smart little mare, not altogether unlike my juvenile recollections of the famous "Brunette," and as I purchased her from a man of the name of Fisher, I christened her "Kate Fisher," from the celebrated mare whose untimely end moved even the great Thunderer to forge a bolt against steeple-chasing, as conducted in Limerick—a *brutum fulmen*, as it proved. This little affair being arranged, I rode back to Central, leaving with regret the lovely valley of "South Clear Creek," encompassed with its pine-clad mountains, and overlooked by the bleak range where the snow is perennial.

The next day, or next but one, was a Sunday; but notwithstanding this, I regret to say, all things being more or less prepared, the ponies engaged rapidly in accomplishing the feat of eating their heads off—a process not hard to achieve when hay is 2d. or 3d. per lb., and corn 7d. or 8d.—it was resolved to make a start in the evening, and camp out in the woods. I therefore hastily made up my saddle-bags, and bought the few necessaries required, such as flour, bacon, &c.; to which the sanctity of the day was no obstacle, almost every shop being open for business on Sundays equally with week-days : a custom which I found to obtain very generally throughout the entire West; and indeed in Central City the infection had been caught by the bankers and dealers in gold-dust, and great " oneyers " who should have set a better example to the minnows of trade.

What a contrast to the conduct of the Jews, who almost universally keep their own Sabbath in addition to the Gentile feast ! Verily it is a popular fallacy to say the Jews are more greedy for gain than any other nation. The truth is, money-making has been their trade from immemorial ages. They have acquired, as was natural, much ease and facility in their

10

several branches of commerce, and a number of envious, disappointed, and distanced competitors raised the cry that their success was the result of avarice and rapacity, instead of attributing it to its real source. For my own part, I have generally found enlightened Jews the pioneers in all measures of enlightened philanthropy, and measuring their liberality by no Christian standard.

All things being thus ready, we rendezvoused at the ponies' stable to pack the outfit on the backs of these our travelling companions; about which I feel bound to say a word "in limine," as they formed a most important element in the cortège. First came "Bill," a large bay pony, of Indian origin, standing on rather tall legs, but so symmetrical and strong otherwise, that no judge of " points " * could fail to give him credit for great activity and endurance at the first glance ; qualities which he developed afterwards in a most extraordinary degree, proving about the best pony I ever saw for his work. His attractions, however, ended here, as his ears were cropped, a portion of his under lip was " razeed," and one of his eyes was a " quaker," or, in other words, " blind," having been injured by a former

* Point in a horse cannot be defined, as in Euclid, as " without parts."

owner in a rage, at his refusal to draw: for "Bill"
had his whims and penchants, and, when once he
objected to do a thing, force or coaxing was thrown
away. He was the pillar of our state on this occasion,
being the flour-bearer, and having nearly 300 lbs. of
that commodity, beside a few other "small deer" on
his Atlantean back.

Next came "Jack," a cream-coloured cobby little
horse, very strong and rather showy, having a
fine "rein" and round large quarters, but withal
very lazy; he was said to be a "flat-head" pony,
from the Indian tribe of that name, and, on the
whole, he proved a useful, but not very interesting
member of our comity. Then comes "Jenny,'
a young Mexican mule, rather small, and with
wonderfully spindle shanks ending in little Chinese
feet, which sunk hopelessly in every bog we came to.
I cannot praise her very highly, but perhaps had the
expletives she provoked by her mulishness been
uttered in Castilian, or "Græser" "patois," she
would have understood our meaning better than
when conveyed to her long ears—

In the oaths of British commerce and the accents of Cockaigne.

She was the bearer of our "batterie de cuisine," &c.,
together with the beaver traps, and made as much
noise as she went along as a whole sleigh team,

having no hesitation in impinging our pots and
kettles against rocks and trees as they came handy
to her. Of "Kate Fisher" I have already spoken,
and will only add that, though no paragon, she
proved a serviceable animal, though not a good shooting pony; she packed any amount of game, and gave
herself no fine lady airs, as she might have done,
being of American descent, while the others were
only Indian.

Having thus disposed of the quadrupeds, let me
say a word anent the bipeds : first, premising that—
filled with adventurers of all castes and classes, as
all western countries in America are, especially if the
region be auriferous—a new element had been added to
the already very mixed and heterogeneous population
of Colorado, by the internecine war between North
and South, as it progressed in its demoniacal career ;
owing to the influx of " Southern sympathizers," to
use the word in vogue in the North, and of some
who had already borne arms for the Confederacy in
the border States of Arkansas and Missouri, and who
having been either discharged or disbanded, preferred a temporary " séjour " in a comparatively
neutral territory to returning to their northern or
eastern homes, and renewing their quarrels with
their neighbours and their own families. Added to

whom were many who, though not strictly partisans of the South, were thoroughly opposed to the policy of the administration, and would, I believe, had they been placed in such a dilemma, rather have joined the Southern cause than been forced into serving in the Federal lines.

To such men—and in the border States, such as Missouri and Iowa they were numerous—these "high latitudes," removed from the atmosphere of war and politics, offered an asylum very similar to that afforded to our proscribed ancestors—and theirs too, perhaps, " quien sabe ? "— by the " Low Countries," with this difference ; that, in this case, free scope was given to the energies of the new settlers, and every avenue of wealth and power was here freely open to their endeavours. Indeed, as a matter of fact, Colorado was filled with men who found home inconvenient during the war, and who were only waiting for a general peace to return to their native States ; some the richer for their emigration, but the majority much the reverse.

My "compagnons de chasse," on this occasion, might all be classed, with one exception, in this category, and were putting in their time here in various pursuits till peace should shine once more on the horizon. First, let me introduce " William " (patronymics had better be suppressed) to your notice. Under thirty, slightly made, and very handsome, with hands as small as a woman's, he was a native of Kentucky; had, when a mere lad, followed an uncle into Texas, and part of the way to Old Mexico, then at war with the United States: a war which, if examined, will hardly present as many extenuating and justificatory pleas as the present French invasion so loudly denounced by all Americans. After that, being of a mechanical turn, he learnt gunsmithing, and having realized some capital in trade, embarked in some general business in a frontier western State; he prospered greatly till the crash of 1857, which swept like a tornado over the whole of this continent, utterly ruined him. The second year of the war found him farming in Iowa, whence he found it prudent to migrate further west; for politics ran high in his neighbourhood, his intimate friend had been hanged almost before his eyes, for refusing to divulge the names of certain neighbours who belonged to an anti-Lincoln Society, called "Knights of the Golden Circle," and he had been menaced himself with pains and penalties if he remained. So here he was occasionally working at his old trade, but generally following the more congenial occupation of hunting and trapping for a

livelihood. He was an exceedingly pleasant fellow,
a little lazy constitutionally, and slightly given to
romancing, but a good hunter when roused to it,
well informed, and naturally well-bred and enter-
taining.

Next comes Miles (a good name for a soldier surely),
fresh from Price's army, where he fought with such
distinction in the Lexington and Springfield affairs,
that he was offered a commission on the field, and
was actually presented by his colonel and captain with
a charger for his distinguished services. His family
being Federals, he, when invalided, struck out for
Colorado, and here mined, hunted, and earned his
living as best he could. He was quite a lad, but full
of talent, being a good histrionic, with a vocation
for nigger minstrelsy and the "bones;" he composed and sung very fair "rebel" songs, which he
chanted most lustily in the Rocky Mountain soli-
tudes, being debarred from such illicit pleasures
elsewhere.

Next comes "Andy," a stalwart Saxon-looking
young fellow, the tower of strength of our party;
as he was a first-rate hunter and woodsman of some
experience, and was besides one of those useful
people of whom you generally find one at least on
every Irish estate by the name of the "handy

man : " our friend Andy was certainly a " handy Andy," for he could do a little of almost every kind of mechanical work, and being good-natured withal, his services were often put into requisition. He reminded me much of the Saxon pioneer, or frontier man, in Crawford's fine group in the Capitol at Washington, who appears warding off a band of armed Indians from a defenceless family of women and children about to be tomahawked and scalped, calm and intrepid in the consciousness of his own courage and power, while—

> The clear soul in his earnest eyes
> Looks thro' and thro' all plaited lies.

He had left his comfortable farm in Iowa for opinion's sake solely, and was sighing anxiously for home and peace—wife and children far away.

My dramatis personæ winds up with an American-Dutchman yclept " John," whose chief hobby was " prospecting " for mines, in which he had some skill and experience : a poorish hunter, he represented the genius of order and regularity in our party, and was thus installed " President of the home department," and general superintendent of the cuisine and larder. We were rather a formidable-looking quintette, each hunter's costume consisting by rights of a rifle, a large cowhorn powder-flask, a bullet and patch pouch, one or two *couteaux de chasse*, and a tomahawk, to cut up large game, blaze-wood on the road for the benefit of posterity and successors, and make itself generally useful in cutting firewood, &c. about camp.

Apropos of costume, I must not forget William's overalls of elk-skin, which he and Andy had tanned and manufactured on a previous hunt, driven thereto by necessity. They certainly were the most useful " continuations " I ever saw ; for whenever string (which is a great item in packing, and must be of the strongest material) was wanted, we used to turn to him and get him to cut a shred off the legs of said overalls, till the latter were soon reduced to the proportions of knickerbockers.

At last we really did get off, in the gloaming of the evening of the 16th of August. After walking some six or seven miles, during which time we only missed our wood-trail once, we struck a stream called " Peck gulch," and camped for the night, as there was some grass for the ponies there. Next morning we rose early, and dispersing through the pines, killed enough grey squirrels and rabbits for breakfast. I confess I had misgivings about eating squirrels for the first time, but am glad I overcame my ignorant prejudices, as I found them excellent—much better indeed than rabbits. A few miles brought us to twelve-mile diggings, now "played out," with the miners' log-shanties all deserted.

A little further progress in an easterly direction brought us to "Mammoth City," consisting of a saw-mill—a quartz ditto dismantled, and a log-hut or two. A Boston Company had commenced operations here on a large and expensive scale, but without any regard to the first principles of mining, or even common every-day economy; the consequence was failure absolute, and everything saleable was being carried off, to leave the pines to their primæval loneliness. There we dined, and in the afternoon, as the weather looked rainy, we sheltered ourselves in a log-cabin a few miles further on, on the spurs of the range, which we proposed to cross in the morning.

Our precaution of stopping proved unnecessary, as the afternoon held up very fine. However, on the whole it was better to cross the range early than late in the afternoon, and so next morning, after losing our trail several times, we at last found ourselves climbing the range in earnest, and soon looking down on the pine-clad steeps below us, from an elevation where nothing but dwarf and gnarled cedars flourished. Our upward path through the timber was literally enamelled with the brightest wild-flowers ; of which being an ignorant admirer, I can say but little, save that they were very lovely and gay : in speaking of these gems of creation I must content myself with very vague generalities, as Horace, when singing of the patrician flower-gardens round Rome, bunched the whole contents of the parterre into a simple " copia narium." * As we emerged from the timber, we found evidences of mining attempts in the prospect holes, and " rasters," a sort of clumsy Mexican machine for grinding quartz ; but everything of the sort had been abandoned. Looking down on the pines below, we were much struck at the enormous extent of the burnt timber, which bears a very considerable proportion to the green, and forms quite a feature in the landscape, the bare grey poles of the former looking wan and ghost-like, till the eye gets accustomed to them.

Presently, after about an hour's very tortuous walking, over ground covered with very short grass and little white and blue flowers of most tiny proportions, the " eager and the nipping air " assured us we were nearing the top of the pass. This was strewn with rocks, over which our ponies walked with

* Omnis copia narium spargent olivetis odorem fertilibus domino priori.

a coolness and *aplomb* that greatly surprised me,
considering the consequences of a false step and the
yawning little crevasses between them. Hereabouts
we got our first view of the Middle Park, which
appeared from hence a confused mass of pine-forest,
mountains, and gorges, with bits of open country
through them, stretching far as the eye could scan.

After another hour's walk along this rocky ledge or
back-bone—of a good breadth, however—we came to
a sort of natural rocky staircase, commonly used, I
fancy, by the deer and elk in their annual migrations
eastwards and westwards; down this our ponies crept
with marvellous surefootedness for about a mile,
when we got on to a lower ledge, and thus by easy
descent in an hour or so we struck the timber on the
other side of the range. Having surmounted the
difficulties of what is called from the outline of the
mountain "the Hog-backed Pass," in a short time we
found ourselves in a deliciously green valley, from the
centre of which flowed a small stream of pellucid
water, which, insignificant as it looked, plied its
watery task till it found a home in the far Pacific: for
the waters of the Middle Park, unlike those of the
north, empty themselves into the tributaries of that
ocean. In this valley we dined, and descending the
spurs of the range, along the same stream, we made

some six or seven miles more before we camped for the night. We killed *en route,* some pine grouse,— a very fine bird, not unlike our own, only larger,— together with a woodchuck, or ground-hog—a curious compound between a badger and a hedgehog, said to be good to eat; but with one accord we declined trying. The stones in the hills seemed to abound with a very curious little animal like a guinea-pig, called, from its peculiarity, here " a dog without a tail."

In the morning we found it had frozen hard, and was bitterly cold. A few miles brought us to the Fraser, a good-sized river, but reduced this year, in consequence of the small snow-fall, to shallow proportions; and as it looked likely to hold trout, I stayed behind our party, and was rewarded by catching two very large fish. I had some trouble in following the track of our party, and was much afraid I had missed it, till after some " tall walking" I found my friends camped by a small mountain brook, engaged in netting, with a very novel kind of seine (willows twisted in the form of the letter V), a deep hole in a stream, out of which they took more than two dozen small trout. Leaving this brook, and proceeding over some small hills in an easterly direction, we struck the Fraser once more, and camped on its banks.

Some of the land we walked over to-day seemed very available for tillage, though now cropped only with the sage-plant, looking much like the lavender-bushes which we see in old gardens, only far larger and more woody, and gnarled. Besides this great staple, we passed a good deal of columbo root, ele-campane, and a sort of bitter bush, something like a gooseberry-tree, which William called wild quinine. In the groves, which are dotted about here and there as no landscape gardener could group them, the undergrowth consisted principally of the juniper cedar, with its berries in all stages of maturity, from green to purple; the latter tasting not unlike raisins.

20th.—The night and morning were again very cold, as indeed they continued to be during the excursion; but the sun soon became very hot, almost overpower-ingly so. Crossing the Fraser again, we struck the Grand River in a few miles. I suspect this name is a corruption of Rio Grande, a common name for rivers in countries of Spanish origin: certainly it is better than one which I recollect well in Jamaica, and which struck me always as a great sin against euphony—"Agua Alta" disguised into "Wagwater!" It is a fine stream, about the size of the Thames at Godstow, but far more rapid, and seemed a favourite haunt for wild ducks and geese. I much regretted then, and on many a subsequent occasion, that I had not brought a shot-gun with me, instead of the Sharp rifle: this I carried specially for bears, as it loaded so very fast, in addition to a three-barrelled affair, of local make, for deer and antelope. We here met for the first time the "sage-hen,"—a grouse, but of noble proportions, and I think heavier than most pheasants. It lives almost entirely on the sage-plant, and if the crop, &c., be removed directly after shooting, it is an admirable bird for the table; if not, the whole flesh becomes impregnated with the flavour of the sage—*un peu trop fort!*

Our course to-day was over arid rolling plains, with the vegetation so burnt up that I was reminded of that forcible line in the " Georgics:"—

> At cum exustus ager morientibus æstuat herbis.

Most of it might, however, be irrigated with apparent ease. In the valleys of the streams or creeks things wore a greener aspect, and where we camped for the night, by Beaver Creek, the grass was abundant. Here we set ourselves to search for game "sign" or spoor; though we found traces of both elk and beaver, unluckily others had been before us, and consequently a change of plans—of "base," to use the jargon of Federal generalship—became necessary; so, on the morrow, William and Miles set out to discover a practicable track to the North Park, which is separated from the Middle by a lower or spur range.

Meanwhile Andy, John, and myself proceeded to explore Still-water Lake, through which the Grand River flows. We found it at last, after a toilsome progress through burnt timber, where your powers of equilibration are continually called into play, and where good knee action is indispensable. It is a beautiful sheet of water, about two miles long, embosomed among the pine-bearing hills, and apparently of great depth. Its sides, as far as we went, were covered with raspberries, which grew on dwarf bushes, and were quite equal to most garden fruit in England; but, unlike those in the States, these were red, while the former are, I am told, generally black. There were also some black gooseberries, but very poor in size. The white and black currant and raspberry are the best small fruit of this region, and grow wild equal to our garden varieties; while here the red currant is a miserable specimen.

Andy shot a very fine beaver in the lake, which we fortunately got and skinned. Generally speaking, when shot they sink at once to the bottom, and if in deep water are very hard to secure. Returning in the evening, I caught some very fine trout in the Grand River, and lost one or two monsters from rotten tackling. In the evening John and Andy posted themselves at an alkali spring, where the elk tracks appeared fresh; but though they saw some elk in the shadowy distance, the light was not sufficiently good to warrant a shot. I returned to camp with the trout. We had a slight shower this evening—in itself no very noticeable circumstance, but I chronicle the weather because, in the first place, meteorology is a sort of privileged ground to an Englishman, forming, as no doubt it does, both in circles polite and impolite, a great staple of his daily conversation, as well as entering largely into his hopes and fears, his plans and arrangements of all sorts; and in the next, because I wish by a daily record to give a fair idea of the climate of these "high latitudes."

22nd.—Finding the flies purchased in this country so badly tied, and the gut to which they were appended so brittle and rotten, that no dependence could be placed on them for large fish, such as are caught in the Grand—varying as they did from three-quarters of a pound to about three, many four, pounds (though we had brought no scales)—we spent the morning in making what we hoped the "trutta" would consider natural flies, but which appeared to me

11

a very poor presentment of any known winged thing. Still, hoping that the principle of "omne ignotum pro mirifico" extended to the genus fish as well as to the genus man, we adopted them boldly, and the result was satisfactory, spite of a severe storm of hail and rain. As I was returning to camp late in the evening, I was fairly pursued by owls, who, I thought, tried to swoop down to the fish, which I was carrying on a stick. Arrived at camp, we found the rain had soaked the buffalo robes which formed our bedding; but with the aid of a good fire we managed to get through the night pretty comfortably.

I haven't said a word hitherto about the grey parrots, or meat birds, which haunt the woods here; and yet, as Cicero said of literary tastes and studies being ever present with their votaries, "pernoctant nobiscum, peregrinantur, rusticantur," so these curious little grey birds, something between a parrot and a jackdaw, were sure to be present wherever we camped, and to "assist" at every meal; almost voting themselves of the party, spite of our occasionally knocking over an intruder with anything that came handy. In the morning they would sometimes scream in a most eerie and unearthly manner, frightening the ponies, till they got used to the dissonance; but what amused me most was to watch one of these birds when about to commit a barefaced robbery, and when perched for the purpose on some bough close to the attraction. If you caught his eye, or he yours, he would instantly begin to look unconcerned, and I am sure, had he been able to talk in our language, he would at once have commenced a conversation upon any other topic than the one great one uppermost in his mind. The conscious guilt, dissimulation, and fear, formed a most imcomparable mélange.

23*rd*.—Andy and I went to the Grand after breakfast, and in an hour or two caught twenty-two large trout, in one of which I found a water-mole. Indeed, I think the trout as greedy a fish as any, though certainly shyer than most; and I may mention that, in these waters, when other baits fail, a trout's eye is considered very telling. Bringing home the fish to camp—a load nearly as great as we could carry—we found our exploring party had returned with a good store of small game. They pronounced the track to the North Park feasible, and amused us with an account of their long chase after bison, which they found on one of the bald mountains between the parks; two of which they wounded, but did not get from want of dogs. These animals are only a mountain species of the buffalo on the plains, smaller and more active, and with more shaggy coats. The day was lovely in the extreme, and so it may be assumed were all that succeeded, unless special mention to the contrary be recorded.

24th.—We breakfasted very early, intending to "make tracks" for the North Park; but alas! the ponies had wandered off towards the alkali spring, or "salt lick," and were not found till the afternoon, during which interval we suffered some anxiety, fancying a party of Indians had come and carried them off, first putting bits of blanket on their feet to avoid traces. Starting late, we camped some six miles off, in a north-easterly direction, at the foot of a high peak, on whose sides I found yellow ochre and the burnt quartz, or "blossom rock" which is such an indicator of gold.

The soil here evidently varied from that we had left, as poplars and balm of Gilead trees were found every now and then in abundance.

25th.—Getting under weigh by seven o'clock, we pursued our course through much broken and burnt timber, which makes travelling very tedious, especially with pack animals, as you have to go zigzagging round the fallen timber in all directions; but at last we emerged into lovely pinewoods, carpeted with huckleberry plants, and breaking every now and then into beautiful glades, full of springs. In one of these glades we camped for the night, and found some black-tailed deer in the neighbourhood, but failed to shoot any. These latter are sometimes called " black deer," from their blue-black colour, and are very wild and shy ; whereas the white-tailed deer are comparatively bold and fearless of men, venturing often into the neighbourhood of settlements.

26th.—The ice was thick in our water-buckets this morning, but spite of the cold, we made an early start, and after toiling through eight miles, more or less, of broken timber, we came to a stream which we surmised ran into the waters of the North Platte. Finding beaver sign in plenty, we determined to camp here for the present, and set some traps; in the evening we got a fawn and also a beaver. John, who went out by himself, did not return to camp, so we fired minute-guns to indicate our position, as if at sea, but still he came not; so I took his place as breadmaker and cook, considering that man is not only defined to be a " featherless biped," " bipes implumis," but also a " cooking animal ; " and I am glad to say that the result was a considerable success. It is true the bread I baked would have created an émeute among the Jeameses and Angelinas of an

English servants' hall, and in the nursery it would have probably been voted highly deleterious. stuff; but we all ate it with much gusto, and I confess to some pride in the work of my hands on the occasion—like Touchstone's wife, "a poor thing, but mine own."

27*th*.—John re-appears with the noon-day sun ; he had fortunately carried matches in his pouch, and having his hunting-knife or whittle, had made himself a fire to sleep by, but for food he had depended on the juniper berries. In the afternoon, thinking we should probably spend some time in the neighbourhood, we built a shanty, roofing it with alternate layers of spruce and pine boughs, which gave a rather pretty result; and as it had several varieties of game hanging round the entrance, I pleased myself by fancying some resemblance between it and Landseer's well-known picture of "Bolton Abbey in the Olden Time." To-day two beavers were caught in our traps.

28*th*.—I set out to-day towards some mountains westwards, which seemed likely to hold elk, bison, and perhaps a stray bear or two. The morning was intensely cold, but long ere noon, Hamlet's wish was realized, and the solid flesh was " larding the lean earth " of the mountains. However, after walking about fifteen or sixteen hours, and meeting no large game, I had to make up my mind to "camp out," supperless; but *en revanche*, I built a fire big enough for a suttee or an auto-da-fè, and passed a comfortable night enough, spite of the cold. I got back to the shanty by about 7 a.m. (29*th*), where I found Andy had killed an elk, and brought in part of it, so the ponies were despatched to bring in portions of the elk, while the remainder was to be jerked or "boncaned" on the spot where shot. Let me here record that my first impression of elk potage was most favourable.

30*th*.—To-day we caught no beaver in our traps, but found one or two legs gnawed off by these intrepid animals in their efforts to regain their freedom. (I learnt subsequently that our system of trapping was radically defective, as the traps should be so set as to drown the beaver at once, and not allow him ever to get on the bank, for if he does the alarm is given to the entire commonwealth.) This gave me a disgust to trapping, especially when a close acquaintance with the habits of beavers, and the sight of their extraordinary achievements in building and colonizing, revealed their wonderful instincts and faculties.

Down this stream, for instance, a succession of dams had been constructed for ever so many miles, in fact far as I could see : indeed these enterprising amphibia covered with their works and dwellings a space of many thousand acres. Here, where willows abounded, the dams were made after the fashion of huge fascines, plastered over with layers of mud, and always placed at precisely the right angle to withstand the force of the current; but whatever the material, be it stones, mud, or brushwood, the beaver makes the best use of it, and I have seen very respectable masonry of their construction. The power of their tails is enormous, and it is with them that they carry logs, large stones, and mud, to give the weight and solidity essential to finish their works. The tail is said to be a delicacy, but I made no experiment myself, having no leader. Their gnawing powers too are well-known, and I have seen in this beaver town many a mountain willow and aspen tree of fully a foot in diameter, cut down by them as neatly as if hewed by an expert axeman. Their houses are round, built of willows, and covered with heavy logs to prevent the wind from carrying off the mud and clay with which they are roofed.

Trappers say that Mrs. Beaver mère occupies the mansion with her family of kittens, yearlings and two-year olds, while Mr. Beaver père is given what policemen call "the key of the street," and has to find himself a "pied à terre," or rather "à l'eau," under the banks of the streams, as best he

can. This doctrine, however, of "separate maintenance," I must repudiate on the part of the
beaver family as inconsistent with the proofs one
everywhere sees of their orderly and well-regulated
existences ; which might, I think, point a whole-
some moral to the sluggard and spendthrift almost
as well as the "inopi metuens formica senectæ"
of Solomon and Virgil. It is said they have multi-
plied considerably since silk hats came into fashion,
for whereas their fur used to command ten dollars
per pound in the market, a whole skin can now
be purchased for about two dollars in the undressed
state. They are wonderfully cunning animals, whenever they have been once trapped, and I cannot
help thinking they hand down traditions of their
experiences in this line, from generation to generation.

31st.—In this colony the beaver were evidently
on the look-out, and so we determined to prospect
for better fields for hunting and trapping ; with
that view William and Miles took the ponies
and set off into the North Park to explore, while
I set out in quest of elk and bear. The latter
animals have generally frequented the North Park
in considerable numbers, as here they found abundant feeding among the huckleberries; but this

dry year that crop has almost entirely failed, and to that circumstance, I suppose, I owe it that I failed to get a shot at either grisly or cinnamon bear, during the expedition : though I saw signs of them in various directions, and fancied I could smell them ; but the want of dogs was fatal. However, when their coverts embrace thousands of square miles, it is a mere chance finding Mr. Bruin at home, without the aid of the " odora canum vis."

The huckleberry is the great undergrowth of the pine-woods hereabouts, and its fruit, varying from the hue of a red currant to that of a ripe black grape, is very pretty, and also good; but I found the trouble of picking them this year was too great—"materiem superabat opus" decidedly. I think they might be introduced into our coverts with great advantage, and have no doubt pheasants would appreciate them, while for rabbits and hares they would make very good "lying." Coming home, I killed the largest skunk I think I ever saw.

Sept. 1.—John and Andy were engaged during this time jerking the elk to make it more portable ; and as this process may not be familiar to every Englishman, I will endeavour to give an idea of it. A number of aspen forks are cut down and planted firmly in the ground, in some sunny spot, and on top of these, some six feet from the ground, are laid a lot of willow or aspen poles, so as to form a framework. Then the meat is cut into pieces of about a quarter of a pound, which are skewered on small willow wands and placed on the frame; under them a slight fire of willows is kept burning, to give the meat the flavour of the wood, and so keep off the flies, which are almost a plague here.

To-day we got a fresh supply of deer and antelope; William bringing in the latter from the Park. I was not a little surprised and pleased to-day at seeing a number of sparrows among the willow-bushes—" Que faisaient ils dans cette galère," I wonder? They were not so fat or saucy-looking as their Johnny Bull cousins, but otherwise had their characteristics.

In climbing up these hills I learnt to appreciate the peasant's excellent counsel to " excelsior "—

> Beware the pine-tree's withered branch ;

for when fallen pines bridge over deep ravines and gullies, the breaking of a rotten limb may cause a similar catastrophe to yourself, or even loss of life; and one may add, in these mountains, beware the withered *tree* likewise, for some of these burnt trees, if you lean your weight on them, will crash down, and you must be careful to be on the right side of the falling pole, or else beware the consequences!

3rd.—Preparatory to a move into the North Park, we shifted our camp about a mile and a half lower down the stream, to see if the beaver there were less on the defensive than higher up; taking up our quarters under a huge spruce-tree, which we found almost rain-proof, the evening being showery. I shot a beaver in a dam this evening, and plunged into the deep water after him, but he foiled me. The rain here was snow in the mountains—pardon the bull— as we saw by their white mantles.

4th.—Andy and William set off this morning into the Park to kill antelope, while I started in the direction of "the range," to see if elk had been driven down lower by the snow there; but the morning was so cold, I could scarcely hold my rifle. On my return, I pulled down about a foot of the dam where I shot the beaver yesterday, with great labour, so well and faithfully had it been constructed !

5th.—On my visiting it this morning, I found the hole I had made beautifully repaired, so I abandoned my hope of getting the beaver by drainage. Andy and William return, having killed four antelope, with one of which the ravens had taken liberties ; during their expedition they had left a fire burning at their camp, and on returning had found a general conflagration, which consumed *inter alia* Andy's coat — a serious loss, when fig-leaves, in the shape of skins, could be the only substitute!

6th.—A general resolution was adopted to-day to move into the North Park, on whose outskirts we were encamped, so, to lighten the load, we partly "grained" and "fleshed" the elk skin; we made a very good "graining" block, by cutting down a smooth aspen tree and placing it on a low fork, the graining knife being a square bar of steel with two handles, which is rubbed along the hide, and takes off the hair and glutinous particles. All round our camp, and indeed generally through the hills, the "killikinnick" plant, which the Indians mix freely with their tobacco, grew in abundance. It is very like the box, only that it does not attain anything near the same size, and bears a lovely little berry, the precise hue of the best pink coral. I think it would thrive in some of our woodlands, in the dry uplands.

7th.—Carrying out our resolution, we "packed," and made an early start, proceeding in a north-westerly direction. After a few miles we got fairly in the North Park, which has a far more legitimate title to the name than the "Middle," as it is a large oval *plain*, comparatively speaking; for though the land rises in places to a considerable height, the view from north to south, and east to west, is hardly

ever much obstructed. I can only give a vague
guess at its length or breath, but think I am within
bounds when I put down the former at about eighty
miles, and the latter at thirty. Its waters flow eastwards; and here that mighty river, the Platte, at
least its northern fork, takes its origin.

After we had made about twelve miles, we
perceived a tent pitched, and some ponies round
it; and a visit proved it to be occupied by no
less personages than the Indian agent for the
Ute nation, accompanied by Mr. Lincoln's private
secretary. They were in quest of the "Ute tribe,"
and had just got into the Park, and were going
back again next day. They had a large suite
with them, but were so indifferently armed that—
"magnas inter opes inopes"—they had no venison,
and were glad of a supply from us. They had
just disturbed a bear among the willows, where
they were encamped; but, I suppose mistrust-
ing their guns, had not even given him a parting
salute.

Proceeding some eight or ten miles further still
in a north-westerly direction over a clear prairie, for
the most part covered with sage brush, and crossing a creek or two, we encamped on the edge of a
small stream, among hills covered with aspen and

cedar, and but little pine-wood. Herds of antelope were seen in all directions, but generally from a mile to two miles distant, and evidently very shy; for this North Park is a great hunting-ground of the Indians, as well as a battle-field, last year having witnessed an engagement between the Utes and Rapahoe nations. The Indian method of hunting makes the wild animals wilder still; for besides shooting them in passes, and watching for them at springs and streams, they are able by their great numbers to drive them in herds through ravines and defiles; whereas white men never hunt in large parties, but generally singly, and consequently scare the game far less. I never tried the plan of hoisting a red flag or even a pocket-handkerchief, and then lying " perdu " till the antelope, attracted like bulls to the strange sight, came circling round — for, like most deer, they are as curious and inquisitive as a turkey*—but it is said to be a very effective mode of " pot-hunting."

8th.—To-day we had the satisfaction of finding that several hundred pounds of the meat jerked with so much care had been spoilt by flies, which are almost Egyptian here in numbers; this was the more provoking as we had carried it so far. In the evening

* Those who have studied this bird will know what an inquisitive nature it possesses.

it rained heavily and continuously, almost reducing us to the condition with which Mr. Mantilini continually menaced his " cara sposa."

9*th.*—The stream we were camped on being joined by one or two tributaries, swelled a mile or two lower down to important dimensions, and was apparently much "used" by beaver, and to-day we secured a very large fellow. Some hail fell, but though so near "the range," the stones were not nearly so large as I saw them on the plains in the summer, where I picked up some fully as large as a musket-ball. Building a shanty of aspen wood, roofed with willow, occupied this day.

10*th.*—Proceeding to examine the beaver traps this morning, without a single gun or rifle in the party, we were stared at deliberately by a large mountain lion on the other side of the stream a few hundred yards off only. He was in no hurry to vamoose, and certainly looked on us as the intruders. This animal has little affinity to the lion proper, but it is akin to the jaguar or panther—called " painter " in parts of the States; it is of great size and power, and, if " cornered," would be a formidable foe.

In the evening I killed a splendid buck antelope, but had to leave him covered up with boughs, as it was some distance to camp. I had misgivings

that in the morning I should find that the wolves or
bears had been feasting on him; but on proceeding
in the morning (11*th*), with a pony, to bring him into
camp, I found him unscathed.

12*th*.—Visiting the traps this morning—I only set
mine occasionally—I found a musk-rat caught in one ;
he was a huge fellow, and the fur appeared to me so
much better than what I had been accustomed to see
that I preserved it, intending to dedicate it to making
a pair of cuffs for some nameless somebody's pretty
wrists. But alas ! " l'homme propose, mais la femme
n'en disposa pas," for the voracious ravens round our
camp, who in our absence held high festival there,
snatched off this little argosy, as well as a companion
to it. The larger beaver-skins were so firmly pegged
into the ground that they tried in vain to appropriate
them ; though I fancy there was a general conspiracy
against our rights of property among the fowls of the
air, for numbers of magpies, who are always at the
bottom of villanies, might now be seen daily round
our shanty.

13*th*.—William and Miles, who had been out some
days, returning with several antelope and beaver which
they had shot, the labour of dressing the hides commenced. As for the beaver-skins, they were simply
stretched in a sunny spot, and secured in the ground

by sharp pegs. Deer and antelope skins have first to be fleshed and grained on a block, then, when free from all glutinous matter, hair, and grain, they are either steeped in oil for several hours (our oil we extracted from the beaver, which, I should say, would be very good indeed for leather and harness), and then given a bath of soapsuds—a process which has to be repeated several times, at considerable intervals. Then they are "pulled out" by hand, and rubbed soft and dry; or else they are immersed in a solution of brains and tepid water, a process repeated, like the oil-dressing, several times, after which they are pulled and rubbed dry by hand. The root of the "Spanish dagger" ("Yucca gloriosa," I think), which is very saponaceous, is often used by hunters in addition to soap, or even as a substitute for it; but here we were too high for that, by, I fancy, several thousand feet. Provident hunters made their own soap in the woods, having the materials, wood ashes and deer fat, in endless profusion at hand.

This evening William returned late to camp, and passing through some willow-bushes near which "Bill" was larrietted, the latter got frightened, probably from being approached on the blind side, and kicked his namesake resolutely; the poor fellow got further entangled in the larriette, and reached camp sorely bruised, and with his shoulder out of joint. We had all heard or read of the true *theory* of putting the shoulder into place again, but knew not the *practice*, and, I fear, caused poor William a world of needless torture in our vain efforts to get the joint into its socket again. Fortunately, we had in camp a little alcohol, which we used to mix with sassafras bark (supposed to be a great attraction to beaver), and administering a little of this did some good in inducing sleep; but other opiates or palliatives we had none. So in the morning (14*th*) it was determined that William, attended by Miles, should push on to the Middle Park, and endeavour to reach the place where the company of soldiers had been sent, as it was hoped and expected a surgeon might be found there; and, if the company hadn't left their encampment, this was much nearer, and more feasible, than a return to Central City. So, putting the invalid on the pony " Jack," as the easiest in his paces, we wished them " God speed," not expecting to see them for many a day; when, what was our surprise a few hours afterwards, to see William and Miles returning; the former, comparatively speaking, all right again, having had his shoulder jerked into place by a stumble of Jack " the Bone-setter's " in crossing some broken ground.

12—2

15th.—This afternoon, spite of slight showers and clouds of menace, I baked me some bread, and rode out, intending to have a long antelope chase; soon, however, it grew dark and overcast, and I was fain to take refuge in some timber on a hill-side. Here I built a huge fire, and, sheltered under my large buffalo robe, bore up as well as I could against the torrents of rain which soon soaked through; and to add to the agreeable sensations engendered by these circumstances, the wolves in the neighbourhood made a perfect " sabbat" of howling, to assure me they knew all about my whereabouts. By-the-by, how poor the word " howl " is in comparison with the Latin expression " ululatus," or even the French " hurlement," any one who has been serenaded by a pack of wolves can testify.

16th.—By morning, snow had succeeded to rain, and not wishing to prolong my stay in the neighbourhood, I saddled " Kate Fisher," and proceeded towards camp, but was tempted to get off " en route," as I saw some antelopes within easy range, and neglected to tie the mare's larriette to a sage-bush. Of course powder and caps refused to do their duty after the soaking of the previous night, though I had endeavoured to keep my rifle as dry as was possible, and a minute afterwards I had the pleasure of seeing

Kate, weary of waiting in the snow, proceeding "sola" to camp, some miles distant, at a long leisurely trot, increased, however, whenever I attempted to near her. This was bearable, and perhaps even a not unpleasant dispensation on such a morning; but presently the buffalo robe, heavy with the rain-fall, dropped off the saddle, and to "pack" this all the way to camp was no laughing matter to me; though, no doubt, a capital joke to her. When I got to camp, all the bile within me stirred by the rebellion and treason of my horse, I had the consolation—which the bad part of one feels in the discomfort of others on certain occasions—to find that the willow roof of our shanty had proved no defence against the heavy rain, and that everything was soaking and pulpy.

The day, however, soon cleared, and we got some antelope before the evening; but, as flour and salt were nearly exhausted, there was a general resolution to return soon to the eastern side of the range; a determination to which the rain had conduced in no small degree, together with the porous qualities of our willow bower; which, in our eyes, was no longer "a thing of beauty," and certainly not "a joy for ever."

18*th*.—This morning we found our spring partially

frozen, but the day being lovely, as usual, I set out for a hunt on Kate; but—confound the cunning jade!—the successful trick she played me yesterday, which I magnanimously condoned, or visited with the gentlest of corrections, stimulated her to fresh efforts in that line, and off she bolted again as I was stalking an antelope; and, though I searched in all directions, I could not make out her whereabouts, but returned on foot to camp in the evening, having killed a doe antelope, which I had been obliged to leave in "statu quo," having forgotten to take a knife with me. Coming back I got entangled among the beaver-dams, and could not find the crossing of the stream, so had to plunge into the icy cold water and wade across. I found the camp empty, every one being out hunting.

18th.—In the morning, after cooking and breakfast were despatched, I set out again to hunt for Kate, whom I found, without much labour; night, and her saddle and bridle—bad sleeping and feeding companions—having superinduced a more sober and reflective if a sadder frame of mind. Returning with my prize to camp, where I had left an affiche stating the loss of the mare—whether stolen or strayed—and requesting any of the party who might return before me, to assist in searching for her, I was startled to find that Miles had come there during my absence, and reversing my "poster," had requested a similar investigation to be set on foot for Jack, whom he had lost from his camping-ground some miles off; he was, however, found in our camp at night—the instinct of these ponies in knowledge of country being quite wonderful; and, besides, I fancied Jack had a platonic tendresse for Kate, for they used to browse sentimentally together in the moonlight nights !

William and John return in the evening with a supply of duck and antelope, and a few specimens of the "sucker" fish they had shot ; the latter struck me as being a good edition of the tench.

19th.—Andy, on his return, gave us an account of some "Rapahoe"* Indians he met, who were scouting for the "Utes,"† their enemies. They were very friendly to him ; indeed I cannot help thinking the Indians are far more sinned against than sinning, and that many murders which have been committed by them on American citizens have been, for the most part, but another instance of "the wild justice of revenge"—seeking victims anywhere, in compensa-

---

* Properly "Arapahoe."

† The North Park is, I believe, debatable territory, claimed by both nations.

tion for long catalogues of oppression, treachery, and fraud. Unfortunately, the blow often falls upon the innocent; the Indian " lex talionis " not discriminating between individuals, but requiring life for life, irrespective of persons.

It is the fashion to abhor Indians, and General Harney, I am told, extirpated them root and branch, killing families indiscriminately, when he was merely sent by the United States Government to protect the emigration across the plains—in itself an aggression in the eyes of Indians. He is universally lauded as a hero in the west; though the authorities at Washington, if I recollect right, punished his conduct on the occasion.

The " Mormons "—who, " on dit," have ever kept good faith scrupulously with the Indians—are beloved by them, and the latter would, I am sure, be a ready instrument in their hands, should any troubles arise between the saints and gentiles: which the influx of miners and prospectors is very likely to accelerate. And though we, as a nation, have no right to boast, yet it is notorious that Indians have far more faith in English honour than in the American article.

To go no further than our own party: had the Indians confiscated our goods and chattels, we should have had no just ground for complaint, for we were knowingly and notoriously trespassing on their favourite hunting-grounds—their own "par droit de conquête, de chasse, et de naissance," and they would have been, according to their code, quite as much justified in taking the law into their own hands, as an English squire would be in prosecuting a poacher. Yet sure I am that if a small party of Indians had attempted to "lift" our horses, or make prize of our guns or traps, the Americans of the party would have at once considered this a declaration of war, even " al cuchillo;" then I must perforce have taken my stand with them, if only for dear love of life. Hinc illæ lachrymæ!— and from causes, such as this imaginary one, arise those fearful frontier feuds, the unjust origin of which on the part of the whites is often forgotten, or conveniently ignored.

Indeed, the whole history of this vast territory is nothing but a chronicle of utter defiance and invasion of Indian rights; the Government every now and then making feeble efforts to do justice, and offering compensations, liberal perhaps in their eyes, but odious to the Indian mind, which is ever rankling with the keen sense of wrongs he can only attempt to revenge in his fitful and impuissant way.

19th,—In the morning I found myself rather the

worse for my cold plunge when more or less heated, and in the absence of a medicine chest, went in quest of the balsam fir, whose gum is the hunter's specific for all the ills that flesh is heir to. Colds and coughs, and even internal complaints, it is said to cure by a healing magic all its own; while I can testify that for cuts and bruises, when mixed with deer's fat, it forms an admirable salve.

20*th*.—Flour running very short, we were put on siege allowance. All things considered, it was resolved to start for the east on Tuesday next; so, as William wanted to take some fresh antelope hams into Central City, he went out and shot two in a few hours' time.

21*st*.—Wishing to have a farewell shot at the antelope, whom I had rather neglected in my vain pursuits after the bear, I started off on Kate, but failed to stalk any, and missed my shots off her back; though game this morning was very plentiful, only they were in large herds, and in open country.

My boots were now worn to such an extent that, having in view the long back track, it was not prudent to take liberties with them. I had attempted to build on the foundation of the worn soles, with leather cut from the flap of my saddle; but the expedient was only of temporary avail. Nothing

but real "iron-clads" will sustain even a brief campaign among those mountains; and mine, though
built by a very talented French artist, in New York,
with a "solidité vraiment Anglaise," being simply
leather, and unplated, were quite unequal to the contest with the rocks in the hills, and the brush of the
plains. Even when riding, the boot becommes uch
worn by the sage-bush; and for that reason let me
recommend the traveller to have a leather guard
placed in front of the wooden stirrup—it will perhaps
save him a pair of boots and some inconvenience:
I think the Spaniards call the contrivance "tapa-
deros."

22nd.—According to resolve, we started in a north-
westerly direction; as it was proposed—mine being the
dissenting voice—to explore a new route, which some
body had heard somebody declare to be shorter and
better than the route by which we came: and besides,
we were promised the advantage of a worn Indian
trail. After proceeding some ten miles, we found
ourselves quite at fault; but following what looked—
from the configuration of the country—to be the line
of trail through some low hills, we had at last the
satisfaction of seeing before us at an interval of about
a mile or more, two tall peaks, which really bore
some resemblance to gigantic rabbit ears, and gave

the pass the name of the "Rabbit's Ears." An easy descent soon brought us into one of what I may call the side pockets of the Middle Park; and as the evening was advanced, we camped in a pleasant grove, felicitating ourselves on the prospect of a pleasant and short journey homewards.

Nothing could exceed the beauty of the colouring of the low hills we passed "en chemin" to-day; under foot the leaves were many-hued—but a bright scarlet predominated—then the currant and wild-cherry bushes wore an orange scarlet livery; while willows and aspens bore every conceivable tint of yellow, orange and brown, with an admixture of pale green; and then in the high background were the dark unvarying hues of the green pine, forming a frame for the picture.

23rd.—Winding along the narrow valley of a stream, we had some difficulty in getting through fresh and deserted beaver dams. There were bare sandy bluffs on either side for some time, but at last the valley widened, and we came on a large herd of antelopes feeding; Andy, who walked about a quarter of a mile in front to guide the cortége, and act as a picket (for a discipline almost military is necessary in an expedition through these plains, and men and horses soon fall into it), shot one, a fine buck.

The whole of this part of the country is full of alkali springs, and in camping this evening (24th), I allowed Kate to lick up the soda freely, having an idea that horses were the best judge of their own dietary; but in the morning I found my mistake, as she was evidently unwell, generally amiss, and drawn up, with her coat staring badly. However, we proceeded, along a most barren and uninteresting country, winding round high sandy bluffs, and returning anon to the gorge of the stream, which soon expanded into a small river.

Kate lagging behind, I rather inconsiderately urged her on by a blow or two, when she took it into her head to try a short cut to make up for lost ground, and plunged into a deep part of the stream, where the beaver had made a long dam; and getting exhausted, from swimming with her pack on, and in her vain efforts to climb the steep banks, I had to jump in and extricate her. Of course, everything was saturated with water, and ammunition and cartridges fared very badly.

At last we had the satisfaction of striking " the Grand," which here is much larger than when we first made its acquaintance, having been increased by the Fraser and its tributaries, and, I think, some other small streams. It was almost literally covered with wild-fowl of all kinds, including wild-geese. Following the valley of "the Grand" for a mile or more, we camped in good grass, among magnificent willow-trees, and built a huge fire.

25th.—We were still quite ignorant where we were in reference to the hot springs, which we were trying to strike, but we followed "the Grand" for some distance, and then fording it, found a trail leading in a north-easterly direction, which we followed. On arriving at the summit of a wooded elevation, lo ! far below us could be seen the gleam of a white tent, with ponies feeding near it; proceeding further we came on a waggon track, which we followed for a mile or two, and then camped : Miles and I went in a procession of two, to see who were the proprietors of tent and ponies, hoping to buy or beg a few pounds of flour, and to learn the locality of the hot springs.

Here I found what stuff Bill was made of. All day he had been packing a heavy load in the hot sun, yet no sooner did I get on his back, and feel him with my knees, than he started off with grand long strides, making no sort of mistake through that broken land, and thinking no more of his gallop at the end than I would of a mile walk, and with wind so clear that a lighted candle might have been put near his nostrils. Yet he was only a pony, probably not much over fourteen hands two inches, and I was riding him nearly thirteen stone ; and he certainly had eaten no corn of any sort for a long time. How was he bred ? and what is breeding ?

The party who were encamped had come from Empire City, for the purpose of cutting hay in the Fraser Valley, near the foot of the range ; they proposed to pack the hay over the pass on donkies, and had—at least the " bosses "—wandered here for pleasure and bathing, accompanied by their wives. To our surprise we learnt from them that we were close to the springs—not more than two hundred yards off—and that the company of soldiers had departed long ago. When the soldiers set out, it was said the object was to build a fort in the Park, to overawe predatory Indians ; but certain malevolent individuals hinted that the Indian bugbear was conveniently invented to prevent the bold volunteers from having to go eastwards and take part in this desolating war.

Our new acquaintances could not give us any flour to take away, being badly supplied themselves, but kindly asked us to tea, and baked us a loaf to take to our absent friends at camp.

26th.—In the morning, being now comparatively at home, John and William determined to push on to Central, with " Bill " laden with jerked meat, &c.,

which they wanted to convert into cash; while Miles,
Andy, and self proposed to stay a few days longer, and
fish the Grand near our old quarters; so wishing them
" by-by," we started with some venison to the
ladies' bower, proposing to breakfast with them, and
then visit the hot springs.

These latter alone are well worth a visit to the
Park, nor would I have missed seeing them on any
account. Following a stream which runs into the
Grand River, here flowing through a fine gorge
between high hills, a few yards bring you to a table-
rock, from which pours down into a well-worn basin
a heavy jet of water, with a fall of about twelve feet.
Approaching this basin, which is encrusted all round
with a sulphureous deposit, you find the water so hot
you can hardly bear it at first, but after a few minutes
spent, *tant soit peu* unpleasantly in acclimatizing
yourself, you will find it the most delicious warm
douche you ever took.   I confess I could hardly tear
myself away from it, and never felt so invigorated by
anything in my life; it reminded me of the fountain of
youth and health which formed such a feature in the
wild dreams of the early Spanish adventurers on this
continent, not to speak of those of our own great
Raleigh.   Yet these dreams did great things for the
world, even in their " dissipation; " for the pursuit

of the chimera led to the finding of the substance. And who can estimate the blessings we, sober-minded votaries of the actual and practical, owe to the heated imaginations and wild distempered fancies of the fifteenth and sixteenth centuries ?

I had been obliged to dose Kate this morning with a largish allowance of liquefied bacon fat, this being an antidote to the alkali she had swallowed, which had reduced her terribly, and might, if neglected, have killed her. In addition, her withers were galled by packing my load badly, so I gave her a bath, much against her will at first; but once in, she seemed to relish it greatly, and I thought it did her a world of good.

Climbing to the top of the table rock, we found four large wells, by which the warm stream was fed; these are said to have each different medicinal qualities, but I failed to discover much variety in the taste of the waters, and I doubt their ever having been scientifically analyzed. A hunter had discovered these springs some time ago, and consequently, by squatter law, was entitled to them. He sold his claim not long ago to *an* enterprising man—or rather *the* enterprising man—of the territory, Mr. Russell, for the sum I think of 1,000 dollars, about 204*l.* English. That gentleman has already commenced a waggon-road from Empire City over the range, of which some six miles are finished, and though the work languishes from want of funds, it is said Eastern " greenbacks " will come to his aid soon ; more especially when it is generally known that a road carried through the Park will be a much shorter route to Salt Lake and the Pacific than *viâ* the Cheyenne pass.

Should it ever be my fortune to revisit these whilom haunts of Indian savagery, I shall expect to see these " hot springs " as fashionable in their way as Spa and Homburg, and I am pretty sure gambling will be carried on with as much avidity ; for surely may they say with Juvenal, of this country,—

Noste
Nos facimus fortuna Deam, cœloque locamus.

In the afternoon we made some nine or ten miles through a lovely country ; but owing to carelessness in extinguishing fire, many miles square had recently been burnt, and trees and shrubs were even yet smouldering in places.

27th.—Moving to an old camping-ground on Fraser River in the morning, we had the pleasure of meeting two hunters who had unfortunately lost their powder early in their trip, and were consequently as anxious to see meat once more as we were to taste flour, so we had no difficulty in making a good exchange.   They had been prospecting for a great bed of virgin copper, which one of them had found a year or two ago, but never could regain the spot. In the afternoon I fished down the Fraser, but caught only one fish,—a fine trout weighing, I think, over 8 lbs. ; other rise, strange to say, I had not, and Andy and Miles were not even as successful as myself.

Our friends the hunters must have left a fire in their camp unextinguished, for presently, as I was fishing down stream, I heard a sound as of distant artillery, and saw a black pall of smoke advancing rapidly towards the river, while behind it a thick wall of red lurid flame came surging along; reminding me—by what mental link I am unable to say— of those vast hosts of Attila which swept the Roman Empire with a besom of fire. Fortunately the wind blew the fiery column away from our camp, and besides, the broad Fraser intervened ; but as the fire crept along one bank of the stream, willows disappeared before it, crackling like dried weeds. In the evening it had gained a wooded hill near us, and the effect of the flames was very grand, obscuring the nearly full moon, which was climbing the sky behind that hill.

28th.—We moved on to the Grand to-day to fish, but the season for the gentle art was evidently on the wane ; nevertheless I caught five splendid trout. Andy was unlucky, but Miles got two fine fish. These trout are evidently salmon-trout, " salmo ferox," having quite that flavour, and the colour of the salmon besides.

Having to return some distance along the river, I found the miserable condition of my boots very annoying; indeed, as Sheridan said of the man who was being conveyed by porters in a bottomless sedan-chair, " Save for the dignity of the thing," I might almost as well have walked " nus pieds: " and yet there was a good deal in that " almost," and I must not be ungrateful to the old coaches.

Apropos of stories, every one knows the old " Joe Miller " of the gentleman at Bath, who inquired for a well-known beau there (perchance the " Nash " himself), and was informed by his valet that he had been " dying" * for several hours, to his infinite consternation. Well, a similar shock was given me before I started: on my inquiring for a man I knew at Central, and being told he was " burying," I concluded sudden calamity or pestilence had been busy with his household, and tried to compose my countenance to befit so sad and solemn an occasion ;† but was pleasantly relieved by ascertaining that the word

---

* At Lexington, Kentucky, I read the sign of a dyer with this facetia on it: " I live to die, and die to live."

† Vultu ad mœstitiam composito.—Tacitus: *Annales.*

here referred to picking currants and raspberries in the woods—a very popular institution, like "nutting" among us.

29th.—Snow fell in the morning, and the weather was biting cold; but in utter defiance of all piscatorial *convenance,* as well as our experience of the last few days, we *would* fish. The result of the three rods was nil; indeed, I think I only hooked a single fish. Snow fell pretty thick during the night, but the cold had sensibly decreased.

30th.—The morning rose fair as could be, but snow lay everywhere when we started for the range; though by the time we made the second crossing of Fraser River, it had almost disappeared, save on the range above us. Following the track by which we had entered the Park in August, we made some six or seven miles beyond Fraser, and camped very near the commencement of the range proper, where timber ceases. We did not propose to venture over the Hogback again, but to go round by an easier pass, over which waggons had actually been dragged by cattle— a road longer, it is true, but much safer; and once the range surmounted, there would be a good road, we knew, *viâ* Gold-dirt City to Central.

Oct. 1st.—We had some slight trouble in finding our way over the range, as the snow lay a foot deep in

places, and the wind revelled without one check on the
top, blowing about the dry snow like dust; but, once
in the timber on the other side, we came to a good
road, and soon struck the Boulder stream, emerging
ere long into a fine valley, where a cattle ranche had
lately been established, under, I should think, very
good auspices, for the valley seemed very grassy, and
a beautiful stream flowed right through its entire
extent.

A small railed-in enclosure here marks the spot
where a hunter and trapper had succumbed to small-
pox, as he was returning laden with peltry. He had
caught the disease from the Indians, among whom it
appears in a virulent form, and had died here (probably from neglect in a great measure) almost within
sight of his goal; a plain board headstone, to use an
Irishism, with a lead pencil inscription, which the
dryness of the climate preserved intact, told the sad
story.

A few miles further brought us to the mining town
of Gold-dirt, which once promised great things, but
is now all but deserted. However, there is one very
flourishing mine there still, in which the Governor of
the territory has, I believe, a large interest. Here
we met a very warm and friendly reception from an
uncle of Andy's, who had, like his nephew, forsaken

a comfortable farm in Iowa, and sought his fortunes out here till "the troubles" were over. I had fortunately preserved, by freezing at night, three very large trout, which astonished these good folks not a little, as they had never seen anything of the sort before.

2nd.—Next day we made our way to Central City, which is only some eight or nine miles distant, passing through several villages, which showed evident signs of the chequered fortunes of mining life.

And here ends this episode in my visit to these western countries—very uneventful, it is true, but interesting to me, as every new phase of life would be, and I hope not wholly the reverse to those who have accompanied me in spirit. The country we travelled over possesses this additional circumstance of attraction, that in the probable course of human events there is little reason to doubt that ere long these wild haunts of the bear, the bison, the elk, and the antelope, will be ringing with the sounds of civilization, and man the contriver ($\pi\epsilon\rho\iota\phi\rho\acute{a}\delta\eta\varsigma$ $\ddot{a}\nu\eta\rho$) will replace man the hunter, as the latter is now elbowing out the Indian, so long lord paramount of these wildernesses.

Since writing these pages I have been struck by the recollection of an old school custom, which rises

to my memory as vividly as if I had but lately
emerged from those golden days. We of the sixth
form used to be allotted, after the Rugby fashion,
separate rooms, ostensibly to foster the more arduous
cultivation of the Muses—who, like modern girls, are
supposed to respond best to ardent vows in bowers
secluded from the profane world ; but though I will
not say that the liberal arts suffered by our dignified
privacy, I *do* know that whist, conviviality, and
general good-fellowship were much promoted by
the arrangement of " studies." On Saturday night,
one of our number invariably gave a supper-party to
his form, after which singing songs was the order of
the evening; and though many ditties had great runs,
none, I think, was so popular as one which, after
a preamble that " some loved to roam o'er the dark
sea's foam," and do several other equally irrational
things, declared the singer's and the whole chorus's
choice was " a life in the woods ! "

Now, I cannot help wondering if any of our warblers
have ever carried out in life the vows they then made
in song; but I must suppose not, as such a chance
falls to few Englishmen, unless their fortunes (or the
want of them) carry them to America or Canada ; yet
in this western country the thing is so easy, and
withal so healthful, and inexpensive, and fascinating,

that I hope I may be successful in persuading some to try it, as I can assure those who do, that it will fully repay them in increased health and energy, and in the satisfaction of having made one step out of the ordinary groove of tourists in a land where cockneys and their ways are utterly unknown.

On returning to Central City I found that an immense excitement had arisen about the Bannack City mines, situated several hundreds of miles north of this place, and beyond Salt Lake City; from this small town alone it was calculated that 500 able-bodied men had "stampeded" thither, and from other parts of the country there had been a similar exodus. Notwithstanding this drain, however, the signs of progress were visible everywhere: new mills were rising fast; brick buildings of good proportions were elbowing out the old wooden and log fabrics; Denver had connected herself with the California telegraph, and Central, not to be behindhand, had linked itself to Denver; and the Mint in the latter place (of which I spoke in some respects unjustly) had actually started into life: the Stars and Stripes waved over a decent edifice of brick, which was actually commencing, or about to commence, business; its chief being a Mr. Lane, own brother to the famous —or notorious—"Jim Lane" of Kansas, senator, partisan, statesman, warrior, and——I leave friends and foes to fill up the hiatus as they please.

Volunteering, too, was going on at a great rate, and various stimulants, besides large bounties, were freely administered in the form of placards, to rouse the public appetite for the Colorado cavalry service. One of these *affiches* struck me as so original that I copy it verbatim :—

" Old Top, are you on it? Come in out of the Draft! Enlist in the Cavalry! Charge round on a brave horse, and show the world that you are no sardine! The 1st Colorado Cavalry, *alias* ' Pet Lambs,' *alias* ' Drathers,' cannot be beat in this or any other country. They have been tried, and fill the bill to a ' T.' Why will you waste your sweetness on the desert air, sweating your life away by daily labour, when your country needs you, and will give you your regular old advance pay and bounty, to say nothing about the good clothes and square meals : regular old hotel fare you will get! You will be mustered out in one year with the regiment, and get the same bounty as if you served three years! Come up to the office, and see us. Take a United States smoke, and get acquainted with the boys ! "

Having been informed at the Denver P. O. that a business letter which I expected had not arrived (though it turned out to have been lying in the office all the time), I had no alternative but to write to my agents in New York, and await an answer with as much patience as I could muster; but as I did not fancy a long stay in Denver, I rode back to Central on a perfect little hunting pony I had purchased, and persuaded Andy and Miles to recross the range, and spend a few weeks more in the Park.

As we got to "Boulder Ranche" the weather, lovely up to this time, looked, as the nigger in the minstrelsy says, very "omnibus," and flocks of brants, and tiny "snow-birds,"—sure heralds of a storm,—warned us back: but in vain. We thought we had immunity from heavy snow till Christmas at least, as the Indian summer was bound to last till then, according to the reckoning of all weather-wise people; but by the time we reached Stillwater Lake, there was considerable snow on the ground, and it was still falling fast at intervals; the weather intensely cold: in fine, there we were snowed up, apparently, for the winter, with small prospect of trapping beaver, as the ice was half a foot thick on the Grand, and there were at least two feet of snow, after a few days, on the ground.

Fortunately, there was a magnificent herd of elk—upwards of a hundred, I think—round the hills near the lake, and we each of us killed one, so there was no fear of starvation; but in hunting, I had the misfortune to freeze one of my feet badly, and not feeling it at the time, had neglected to thaw it out in cold water, and thus became completely " hors de combat." I fully resolved that, so soon as the prospect brightened ever so little, I would make a run for it, at all hazards; and accordingly, having got rid of most of my impedimenta, though burdened with two elk hides, the " opima spolia "—at least, one of them—of the finest animal I ever saw, the lord and ruler over that large herd of between one and two hundred, and a magnificent head and antlers I intended to bring home as specimens, I set out with my ponies (who had subsisted for the last ten days on a miserable pittance of frozen grass, procured by pawing off the superincumbent snow) for Fraser River, hoping there to find some of the hay-making party, who had a log-cabin there; but though the distance was not much over fifteen miles, it took me a great part of three days to accomplish it, and then the ponies were rather exhausted by their efforts.

I shall not easily forget my feelings of relief and thankfulness when I saw the blue smoke curling upwards from the log-hut of the hay-makers, assuring me that, at any rate, I should find warmth and shelter, and probably assistance in crossing the range; and besides there was a large stack of hay for the ponies, and shelter for them, too, on its lee side.

Had this party left the park, as I much feared they would, driven off by the premature severity of the season, my situation would have been unpleasant in the extreme ; for if the passes had not been travelled over since snow began to fall, the depth would probably have rendered crossing a service of considerable danger, and my ponies, in their half-starved state, were not equal to any great efforts, nor could I give them much assistance.

True, I carried a good supply of meat with me, and a little bread, but my stock of the latter was getting very small, and I had no cooking utensils. However, now, thank God, all apprehensions on these grounds were removed.

Entering the log-hut, I found two of the hay-makers still there ; but the principal " bos," or chief of the party, whom I had met but a few weeks before in the highest health and spirits at the hot-springs, had missed his way close to this log shanty in a heavy snow-fall, and though every search was made, his corpse could not be found : for that he perished from the effects of the cold was incontestable.

After waiting three days here, a slight thaw set in, and as the "trail" by Empire City had been kept open more or less, I found no great difficulty in making that village in one day, with the aid of a guide, though the distance was about twenty-five miles. Arrived there, my ponies were my first care, and I had the mortification to find that hay had mounted, in consequence of the cold "snap," and the blockade of the roads, to the enormous price of eightpence per pound, and was so scarce at that figure, that I failed in securing a mouthful for my unfortunate nags, though I got them a handful or two of maize at proportionate rates.

The weather ever since has been lovely and genial, and on the eastern slopes the snows have melted away; and were it not for my frozen foot, I would be glad to spend another few weeks in that grand Middle Park, and see how Andy and Miles, who had voted themselves a "fur-company," were progressing in their efforts to collect wolf and fox skins, and mink and martin, of which there were several in the neighbourhood of our camp.

I hope it will not be deemed superfluous, if I add a few lines on the subject of public sentiment in Colorado with reference to Europe.

It may be deemed a matter of but slight moment

what people think on these subjects at a distance of
upwards of five thousand miles, but if it be true that
—spite of the desolating wars which now ravage
so large a portion of the universe, and the dark war-
clouds which lower over the remainder—the world is
being more and more swayed by the dominion of
thought and moral power, the opinion of a very
intelligent and advanced community such as that
which occupies Colorado and its neighbouring territories, cannot fail to carry with it something of
interest, and something also of weight, even if un-
acknowledged.

On my first arrival here I felt that I almost
belonged to a hostile, rather than an allied and a
friendly, power. The Federal party were openly
crying out for war with England, and retaliation
and privateering were among the milder measures
advocated. Every blow inflicted by the *Alabama*
and *Florida* on American commerce was appraised
at its fullest value, and compound interest, with
a handsome bonus besides, was to be demanded
from " perfidious Albion."

It is true, the Southern party was more friendly
disposed; but its attitude was more one of anxious
hope mixed with much apprehension as to the policy
of foreign powers, than of confidence or expectation;

and this party, though strong here, would not, of course be very outspoken under the existing pressure of armed force, espionage, and provost-marshals at every turn. Four months have, however, produced quite a revolution in public opinion, which is almost as mobile as the Athenian of old. Earl Russell's speech at Blair-Athol is warmly applauded, and has thrown any amount of oil on the troubled waters of popular indignation; while the attitude of our Government, and the changed tone of part of our press, have worked wonders in soothing the vanity of the ruffled public mind.

I think Lord Palmerston would find here a fair share of support against any candidate for the premier-ship that is likely to arise among the narrow lists of "possibles;" though, of course, no one conversant with American sentiment, can doubt for a moment that Bright and Cobden are the men whom Northerners would fain see at the head of England's councils.

But the effervescence which lately boiled up so fiercely against England, is now turned against France, and that with far more earnestness and meaning. I have no doubt that, were the war to close soon, a small army of filibusters would be raised here, in behalf of what is deemed the popu-lar party in Mexico, and with the determination of driving the French into the sea; it may be that companies of individuals will attempt some mad demonstration of the sort, even before that much-wished-for epoch arrives: indeed, I have heard some indistinct rumours and mutterings of the kind already.'

It is astonishing how deeply that sop to the gigantic vanity of the Americans, the Monroe theory, has penetrated all minds; and there can be no doubt that, in spite of the enormous inducements for people to remain at their peaceable callings and avocations in this country, armed men would rise as from the fabled dragon's teeth, from the very ground, and from under the ground, in vindication of that very doubtful, and, as it appears to me, irrational doctrine.

There is, I think, no particular love for Mexicans in the sentiment; except that nations, like individuals, are perhaps disposed to feel a patronizing affection for those whom they have well "whipped," and that, as in younger life, masters will make it a point of honour to fight for the fags whom they themselves bully. But it is the notion of interference and meddling, as they deem it, which they are in no mood to brook; and, though patient and forbearing under what they consider a national insult, it is—

> The vigil long
> Of him who treasures up a wrong.

14

CHAPTER IV.

Sed revocare gradûs superasque evadere ad auras,
Hic labor, hoc opus est.—VIRGIL.

No warmth, no cheerfulness, no healthful ease,
No comfortable feel in any member:
No shine, no shade, no butterflies, no bees,
No fruits, no flowers, no birds, no leaves. No-vember.
HOOD.

HAVING said all I know about Colorado and its cities *in esse* and *posse*, I suppose the natural course would be to write " Finis," after the fashion of the school literature of my day—a word which was generally hailed with more delight than any other in the volume; as I find that I must perforce retrace my steps, instead of extending my driftings into New Mexico and from thence *viâ* California to Old Mexico, returning to England by the West India Royal Mail Company's route from Vera Cruz, or Tampico,—a fair vision of travel which I had pictured to myself, with anticipations of pleasant excitement from the *feræ* and *feri* indigenous to this line of country, and of obstacles all surmounted successfully with the ease and *aplomb* with which "raspers" and "yawners" are sailed over, under the genial influences of a wood fire, and a magnum of '34 claret, earned by hard work in the shape of a good day's sport with hounds, or in covert, when, if ever it be granted to sing in chorus with Tom Moore, the Pôte of Ireland, but now, I believe, more especially and locally of Westmoreland Street, Dublin—

If there be an Elysium on earth it is this—it is this !

For—pardon the digression—is there not there the positive happiness of a good dinner done justice to, the memory of which, like that of a good deed, is so delightful a retrospect ?—and sure Paley, no mean authority, "non sordidus auctor," places the nerves of felicity in the gastronomic region ! Is there not, rising in the scale of the beatitudes, " The sober certainty of waking bliss" in that postprandial forty minutes which innovators denounce as "barbarous," because not "continental," and because their lukewarm spirits could never rise to the delights of the occasion ? Beyond, are there not the more chastened pleasures of the drawing-room, to which you gain access by no " Al Shiraz" bridge, but through an easy *portière*, and where—

Rear'd by each grace, but still to be
Man's household Anyadomene,

woman sheds her fascinations, increasing and in-
tensifying in their magnetism with the circling hours,
like the odours of the night-blooming Cereus. And
if this be not enough to fill your cup of happiness,
is there not, even after that planetary influence has
been withdrawn from your horizon, the half-hour of
half-hours in the smoking-room with the few " âmes
d'élite," when, with nerves in harmony with all ex-
ternal things, hope and memory speak only in pleasant
tones, and the world appears for the time, as we are
told in the good book 'twas originally created—a very
good one ?

May this long ramble be forgiven me, in consideration that I write in a land where such hearty
pleasures exist not, and that, as dancing music sometimes fairly gets into the heels of some charming
terpsichorean, the very mention of the subject inci-
dentally has positively run away with my pen. Having
then to return to the east *via* " *the* River," as the
Missouri is invariably styled west of its banks—
much as the Egyptians talk of the Nile, or as the
Chaldæans did of the Euphrates—it has occurred
to me that, having dwelt somewhat tediously on the
trip to Colorado, I might improve the occasion by

saying a few words about my experiences on the road home, in the hope that my discomforts may prove pilots to any future mariner on these stormy land-seas.

When I escaped from the snows of the Middle Park in the lightest of travelling order, having been obliged to abandon even " ce superflu ci nécessaire," I had requested my friends at the haymakers' shanty to pack a magnificent fifteen-point elk-head with the hide, which I was most anxious to preserve as a hunting trophy from the Rocky Mountains, on donkeys, over the passes of " the range," and in consideration of this future service and past hospitality, had presented them with a very fair guerdon. They promised to send them to Denver within a fortnight—a period which I deemed only sufficient to cure my frost-bite, which looked rather serious, to enable me to sell my ponies, and make all other arrangements for departure. Besides, I was assured by the weather-wise and old denizens of the country, that such a cold snap as we had just experienced was as exceptional as the visitation of a comet; and I therefore looked forward rather confidently to a warm, sunshiny journey across the plains, with vegetation improved by the snowy shroud in which it had lain perdu so long, and the roads in their normal condition of hard excellence, once the effects of the thaw had subsided.

To strengthen these delusive hopes and anticipations, I had not been two days in mine inn at
Denver, ere the weather became genial and balmy
as in our warmest days of May or early June.
True, the ground was covered with snow nearly a
foot in depth, but it was fast yielding to the hot
rays, and the labourer might literally have obeyed
the Virgilian precept,

Nudus ara, sere nudus,

had he been so minded, and the "code costumier"
permitted such an innovation. The ravens—here
almost as numerous as crows—were uttering guttural
jubilations to be interpreted by none save Teutons;
and all the animal creation was rejoicing in the
change from "frigidum sine" comfort to "calidum
cum," when lo! as unexpected as unwelcome, another
cold snap, almost equal in intensity to the former,
came on, and with it more snow, though not in any
great quantity or volume. I had turned out my
quadrupeds on a ranche near town, as to keep them
at livery at the rate of 7s. 6d. per diem apiece
far exceeded my financial resources, especially when
nearly all the grooming they got had to be performed
"in propriâ," and not by deputy; and on my visiting them the second day of the cold weather, I found
poor "Kate Fisher," who had suffered greatly from

cold and starvation in the park previously, *nearly* a subject for the kennel—she must have become so *quite* in a short time if left there; while my other pony, whose early life had probably been spent among the Indians, was also in rather a dilapidated condition, though he bore the chilly influences better than his companion. Their state resolved my determination. I had entertained an idea of purchasing a light conveyance of some kind, and driving back this pair (though no more matches than Smike's shoe and boot were "a pair")—a course now impossible for some time, without morally incurring all the pains and penalties of Dick Martin's act. To keep them in a stable at existing rates till condition could be built up, was not to be seriously considered, so I sold them right off at a figure which transcended my previous experiences of "alarming sacrifices" in horseflesh; and as the overland stage company could not promise a seat for some time, I took a passage in a team proceeding to Omaha next day, determining to wait no longer for the advent of my promised antlers, and "opima spolia."

I knew something of my *compagnons de voyage,* and we made up our minds to urge our vetturino to make the quickest tracks he could eastwards, as we argued that every mile by which we increased our distance from the Rocky Mountains, would bring us into a better climate, and make travelling more tolerable. *L'homme propose!* instead of diminishing, the cold and snow seemed to follow us in greater force over the dreary plains, which looked Arctic in their frozen wretchedness. Following the Platte river, instead of taking the "cut off" road, as in summer, and making but short journeys owing to the extreme cold, we passed the old Indian trading posts which marked the first settlement of this territory by the hardy trapper and hunter, and whose names, such as "St. Vrain, Cache la Poudre," and "Vasquez," told of their foreign origin. These mud, or adobe buildings have been called "forts," and retain their nomenclature; though apparently strong only against the attack of Indian arrows. They are now ranches for the accommodation of the "pilgrims" going and coming, and I think "*Fort à lice*" would be a more appropriate designation for them, as I am convinced their borders are not free from those invaders.

This dreary monotony of slow travelling, and miserable accommodation at night, in which all our efforts were necessary to save ourselves from freezing, varied only by a running accompaniment of lean and hungry Cassius-like wolves, who kept

at a distance barely respectful, continued for some
five or six days, when we encountered a "tour-
mente" of snow, which was not only extremely
disagreeable but withal dangerous. At the time
we saw it coming we were some miles from any
ranche, and the danger to be dreaded was that we
might miss the track, unmarked and undistin-
guished in any way save by the proximity of the
poles of the telegraph (that great Memnonian harp
of the 19th century), which rose not far from the
road all the way from the Missouri river. I shall
never, I think, forget the way in which the wind,
careering with unchecked violence on those vast
plains, lifted up huge clouds of the frozen snow,
like so much dust, and buffeted us with it till men
and horses were well nigh blinded by the fury of the
assault.

An old mountaineer and myself had to take
charge of the waggon, as the "Bos" and the rest
were fairly knocked out of time by the storm and
cold, and had subsided into blankets and buffalo
robes. And indeed, had not the horses, by a marvellous instinct, persevered in following the road, and
faced the storm in an undaunted manner, I can
hardly say what the results might have been; for
latterly the telegraph poles—our sun, moon, and

stars—were undistinguishable, and to have wandered
out of our course would, I think, have proved fatal
to some at least of the party ere the storm had subsided. At last, however, the gallant pair, worthy of a
mural crown, for saving so many " citizens," brought
up at a small ranche, which, but for their sagacity,
we might easily have passed unnoticed. Here we
found a number of storm-stayed unfortunates, condemned for their rashness in crossing the prairies in
such weather to learn something of the amenities of
a middle passage, or an " emigrant hold," ere the
government had taken the care of these poor victims
to shipmasters' greed properly in hand.

Fancy fifty or sixty rough specimens of humanity
crowded into a small room, heated by one or more
stoves, on which all are trying to cook their rations
of the unclean animal, bake their bread, or " biscuits "
(as the Americans call the hot rolls which they so
much affect at every meal, to the manifest injury of
the digestive machinery), and to boil the coffee with
which the *rudis indigestaque moles* is washed down.
At the end of the room is a small bar where the
ranchero stands, at the receipt of custom, dispensing
liquid poison liberally in return for shin-plasters and
" currency;" the effect of which is soon manifested
by the most damnable iteration of awful blasphemies

uttered by thick tongues, and more especially the constant repetition of that most sacred name which, to English ears, is most offensive, even where calloused more or less by use. Snow brought in by every incomer melting in the hot and stifling atmosphere, together with copious expectorations, had reduced the mud floor to an unpleasant consistency; yet here you must make your bed and woo nature's sweet restorer, unless you have been lucky enough to pick out a sheltered spot in the large shed which serves for a stable, and have a sufficiency of robes and blankets to mock the cold! This description gives an idea, though an undercoloured and inadequate one, of the *agrémens* of our *trajet* per waggon across Nebraska for some seven or eight days more; though in some ranches the features of the case were worse, in others better, according as the dimensions were ample or contracted. At the stage stations, however, comfortable meals were procurable for the not very high sum of 3*s*.; and in one or two of the ranches better night accommodation was procurable, if you were early in the field, and willing to pay for " luxuries."

Nor, indeed, was the case of the crowded overland stage company's coaches much better; as the roads prevented rapid locomotion, and the drivers, following the example set by nearly all classes of employés throughout the States, were preparing for a general strike, and were indulging in what was called here a "tear,"—which, translated into American, means that they were very "tight,"—in plain English, they were drinking harder than usual, and were reckless of consequences; under these circumstances, the mails were delayed most unconscionably; the drivers, unless handsomely bribed by the passengers, "laying over" on the score of weather and danger !

Thus, though the cold moderated considerably, matters stood till we got within some twenty-five miles of Fort Kearney, and as I gained a glimpse of Buffalo in the distance by climbing on to the roof of a dobee ranche, I determined to relieve myself from the unpleasant congregation of "bull-whackers" and the very mixed multitude in which we had got intricated by the storm; so when the teamster sounded his note of preparation in the early morning, with the usual formula of "All aboard for Omaha, or the River !" I took out my property and wished him *bon voyage :* to our mutual satisfaction, no doubt, as he had pocketed the fare for the entire distance (no American "parts" without strong pressure), and the loss of some two hundred and odd pounds of live and dead weight is no small consideration, when the snow is deep and the way is long; and I was sick *ad nauseam* of the conveyance.

I have but little to say anent buffalo-hunting, as, though I tried the brutes on four different occasions, wasting much energy and caloric on them, the result —except in the amusement I derived from contemplating their huge ungainly forms—was nil. The last time I made my essay with a regular semi-professional hunter; but he was even less fortunate in his stalks than myself, as I always got a few long shots, some of which ricochetted and thudded against their shaggy armour, but perfectly harmlessly, as the range varied from five to eight hundred yards. The fact was, time and place were both unfavourable in the extreme. The cunning beasties had carefully withdrawn from the bluffs and broken ground, when a little dexterity and knowledge of stalking would have brought a hunter within seventy or eighty yards of their whereabouts; at which distance a buffalo ought to be brought to " attention " very readily by one or two shots, when, with a breech-loading rifle or a revolver, you can soon finish the work. Hunting them afoot on the open prairie, where there are no favouring gullies or ravines, is said to be dangerous, as a wounded bull can make a fast and furious rush, and no ordinary runner can avoid their charge

save by a well-directed shot or two at close quarters;
and for that some nerve, and luck too, is wanted.

In the present case, there they were in droves of
twenties and upwards, dotting the level plateau
covered with frozen snow from two to three feet
deep, far as the eye could extend. Generally speaking, they commenced skedaddling like wild-geese in
long single file, ere one could get within half a mile
of them, looking for all the world like small elephants
as they cantered away into the far distance, with their
short tails stuck up in the air like quarrelsome
terriers; then so soon as one drove started, a regular
stampede ensued, and you had to turn your attention
to some new lot of black specks in a totally different
direction, to be probably served in the same fashion
da capo.

Towards sundown, however, you had a better
chance of getting within range, and once, by dint of
much genuflexion and serpenting on the frozen snow,
I got within about 150 yards of a small herd of six,
who saw me most distinctly in my approaches; but
as I salaamed and kotooed in the most abject manner
whenever the watchful taurus turned to stare at me
in his vulgar bovine way, I suppose they thought I
was something too insignificant for notice, and so
suffered me to draw near. When quite satisfied as

to range, and with arrangements for rapid firing as to cartridges, &c. completed, lo ! the cap (not Eley's) refused to perform its functions, and the chance never returned.

The stalker has this immense advantage over the buffalo, if to windward of him, that the latter, if approached sideways, has to make a regular turn of his neck to see his pursuer, owing to the quantity of shaggy hair with which his neck is covered; and I am convinced from what I observed that this position is so unpleasant, that nothing short of a sense of what he owes to his personal dignity and safe keeping would induce Mr. Buffalo to prolong his stare, giving him, as it must, something akin to our crick in the neck.

The legitimate way of hunting buffalo, now universally practised by white and red men alike, is on horseback, and with a revolver, or any other weapon you fancy; but the former is far the handiest, and most deadly at the short range you thus secure.

Your horse, pony, or mustang, however, should be a " hunter " (though not in the sense in which a Symmons or a Potter would understand the term), should have a decided taste for the sport, and an entente très cordiale with yourself, or both may come to considerable grief. I could have got a very

good mount, but the snow was too deep and con-
creted to think of riding hard. My host, the ranchero, a very pleasant person, who to much experience
on this continent added a large stock acquired in the
East India Company's service, and whose wife—Dutch
like himself — was a very bijou of the domestic
virtues and a real helpmate to her husband, such as
is rarely met in these latitudes, wanted me to wait
patiently in his "dobee" till the snows melted,
when he promised me a "big hunt" on the Republican, a stream which runs here some sixteen or
eighteen miles south of the Platte, and where game
of all kinds, including deer and wild turkeys, abound;
but the great uncertainty of the prospect balanced
the reversionary advantages to accrue from a stay, and
after wasting two days and a half in futile efforts to
circumvent "messires les buffes," I got a conveyance
to take me to Fort Kearney, there to await the chance
of a seat in the coach.

While on the subject of "sport," I may mention
that all along the plains here in winter there is good
wolf-coursing; a chasse not to be altogether despised
in its place, though the pace is far from good, and
the "obstacles" absolutely none: unless it be, perhaps, some natural ditch in the prairie, or small
"slue," over which your horse, if worth his feed,

will stride. They hunt them with any number of dogs, from two couple upwards, curs of the lowest degree, but with a dash of pluck and speed withal, and five or six wolves may be killed easily in a day. The small prairie wolf gives the best run; the larger, or buffalo wolf, being a poor runner, maugre my Lord Byron's glorification of the "long gallop:" but his teeth are formidable. The dogs seize their prey by the hind leg, and pin him, while you despatch him with club or revolver; taking care of the "pelt," which has a marketable value of from one to two and a half dollars. The skins make beautiful robes, when properly dressed and trimmed with the tails " au naturel," and look very well on a neatly-turned out sleigh.

The islands on the Platte hereabouts are large and well timbered, and sometimes abound with deer. I found good hare-shooting on one above here, and prairie chickens, which are following the settlements, may be sometimes shot on them.

I would not wish to imply by my unsuccess in this short buffalo campaign, that there is any diffi-culty in getting sport enough for any appetite, no matter how gluttonous. It is true, that every year as the wave of emigration sets westward in increas-ing volume, buffaloes will recede further and further

from the vicinity of the thoroughfares; but it is probable that many a year must glide by ere their vast
hordes will have disappeared from their favourite
haunts on the Republican and Arkansas rivers, and
the vast intervening country now appropriated to
Indians, and long likely to remain in their undis-
puted possession.

Here, or hereabouts, the hunter may find them at
almost all seasons of the year migrating either north-
ward or southward; walking literally in the steps of
their ancestors as faithfully as any ancient Egyptian,
undeterred by the traditionary terrors of the Co-
manche arrow, or the deadlier revolver of his pale-
faced enemy, more cruel in this than his red brother:
for whereas to the red man, the buffalo is not only
meat, drink, and shelter, but also the source whence
he supplies himself with all the artificial wants that
the tide of civilization, reaching even to his borders,
has made imperative, by the sale of the robes squaw-
tanned; the white man kills him too often in mere
wantonness, only using the tongue and hump steak,
if even that, leaving all the valuable carcass and hide
to the wolves and ravens. Indeed, nothing exas-
perates an Indian more than this profligate waste of
game; and I am sure many unfortunate hunters and
travellers have paid forfeit for the wholesale destruc-

tion of buffalo, not many years since, by a well-known English sportsman, who made a long hunting pilgrimage through the Northern Rocky Mountain region.

For my own part, I do not think buffalo-hunting would afford me any very great sport either on foot or horseback, and I have already mentally classed it as hardly on a par with calf-hunting in our own sweet isles of the West; but there is no doubt it does prove to some intensely exciting, and even in summer a good deal of amusement is obtained by larrietting the calves from horseback, or catching the little monsters in your arms—no easy matter—as they go to the water to drink. Many are thus secured yearly; and in the Western States 'tis no very uncommon sight to see a buffalo or two along with a herd of cows. I confess I should strongly object to any intermixture of the blood of the hirsute monster in any herd of mine, as likely to undo all the good effects of years of care and patience, in improving quality of flesh and sym-metry of outline; and I should think the experiments we have already tried with the Brahmin bulls ought to satisfy any sceptical harker back to nature of the impolicy of such a monstrous alliance of beauty and the beast.

All sport requires in its essence some element of

difficulty or danger to give it zest and savour; and
buffalo-hunting combines both, no doubt, to a certain
extent, but in a limited degree.   The "chasse à
pied" is obviously the most perilous; but ordinary
care, good arms, and a tolerable stock of nerve, are
an "æs triplex" which the buffalo seldom can
pierce, and, as hunters usually go in pairs, the risk
becomes small by this division.   It is true, one
occasionally hears of man and horse getting gored
in the conflict, "si rixa illa est, ubi tu feris ego
vapulo tantum!"

But I doubt much whether the bull paddocks of
merry England might not, if carefully explored,
afford an almost equal percentage of danger and
accidents, while to class the "chasse aux buffes"
with pig-sticking in India, or fox-hunting in "the
shires," is simply a chimera of a distempered imagi-
nation.   As a proof of this remark, I will mention
that among the great "lions in the way" are the
prairie-wolf and fox-holes in which your horse may
put his foot when galloping, to the great detriment of man and beast; but these holes, if larger
than our rabbit-holes, are more easily avoided by a
prudent nag with a leg to spare: certainly they are
not nearly so numerous, and I think even "the
Briggs" himself would not be deterred by such a

consideration from rushing to the front if the talis-
manic " tally-ho " had once gone forth, or the cheery
horn had sounded in his ear.

But if the perils of buffalo-hunting are small in
comparison with those incident to other wild sports,
such as pig-sticking and elephant-shooting, there are
certain contingencies to be guarded against in this
chasse, the neglect of which may lead to considerable
inconvenience and discomfort, amounting in some
instances to positive danger. Not the least formidable among these is the risk of being led away by
your sport to regions in the prairie, where, save to
the very practised eye, there is no guide or landmark
whatever, and where every step you take may be leading you further and further away from your camp.
Could the history of these plains be written, it would
be found to abound in narratives of human suffering,
privation, and death, from the " terrible torture of
thirst," and hunger too, full as appalling as the
records of any sea, however " inhospitum." It was
in the great stampede to California in 1847 and 1848
that these horrors culminated ; in those years many
a family of enterprising pilgrims succumbed in their
efforts to reach the Eldorado through this middle
passage, while instances of cannibalism are but too
well authenticated.

The road to the Pacific was then comparatively as
little known as the north-western passage; and it is
averred—let me hope for the sake of humanity un-
truly—that the little light existing on the subject was
turned into darkness by a "smart" Eastern firm,
which actually published a *carte de pays*, leading the
travellers by a route straight indeed as an air-line,
but where the means of subsistence were absolutely
wanting; and as in those days of feverish excitement
and gold delirium few questions were asked, and the
means of contradiction and refutation were scant, the
consequences of this awful misrepresentation became
deplorable.

As, however, hunting camps are generally pitched
near some large river, such as the Arkansas or Platte,
or their tributaries, the inconvenience is generally
limited to compulsory abstinence for a longer or
shorter space of time, as the case may be, if the
weather be fine, as it usually is; but if the plains be
covered with snow, and the thermometer have reached
a low temperature, the situation is far more serious.

The first evening I went out in quest of buffalo I
was very nearly caught in this trap for the unwary.
Following a bull, which I fondly imagined I had dis-
abled from active service, I was only compelled to
desist by the waning of the daylight, which the

snowy surface of the ground prolonged a few minutes in my favour. Guide or landmark there was none ; but as I knew I had been walking nearly due south, it remained to head north, for before reaching the Platte the wheel-tracks of the road must be crossed ; and as there were ranches along it at intervals of eight or ten miles, there were no grounds for fear. I had, however, gone further than I had imagined, and kept on thinking I must be on a wrong course ; but fortunately reason prevented me from changing my direction, as the weight of the probabilities inclined that way : and it proved very fortunate that I did so, as a twelve hours' tramp for a weary man—the only safeguard against freezing to death—would have been rather too serious a struggle with the powers of sleep and numbness to be lightly contemplated.

Having gone on thus for some time, I commenced firing my rifle, till I had exhausted my very last cartridge, but elicited no signal in response that I could hear, though straining hard to catch an answer. After some moments I heard a loud noise in a westerly direction, which, though not like the sound of fire-arms, I could not attribute to any other cause. I have since ascertained it must have been occasioned by the cracking of the thick ice in the Platte. I was on the point of turning my steps in the direction of the sound; but happily I was still cool enough in mind to reflect and resist the impulse, and after a few minutes more of suspense, perseverance was rewarded by striking the wheel-tracks in the road, made by the snow very evident, then after another short interval my ranche was gained, where I learnt that guns of distress had been fired, though I had not heard them.

Failing to get a seat in the overland mail to Aitchison, and the prospect of obtaining one becoming very indistinct, I had to accept the alternative of a drive to Omaha instead; to make my way thence by coach across the State of Iowa as far as St. Joseph, whence the Hannibal and St. Joe Railway led you either to Chicago, *viâ* Quincey Illinois, or to St. Louis by the North Missouri line. There was also another route open *viâ* Grinnell to Rock Island, and thence to Chicago; but as I had some business in St. Louis, I was fain to adopt the former.

The road from Kearney to Omaha lies almost entirely along the Platte, and as its margin is here well wooded, the dreariness of an endless prairie view is pleasantly relieved. Settlements, too, are met with far more frequently than on the western side of Kearney; and though "Dobee" is still king, and rules with undivided sway, Dirt is not so evidently his Prime Minister: in a few little marks of woman's handiwork, such as white dimity curtains at the windows, one sees the touch of a more humanizing nature, linking these outposts to the civilized world and making them kin. Farming, too, seemed to be conducted very generally, and almost every ranche had some land in corn or other crop around it.

Omaha ought, I believe, to be reached in thirty-six hours; but we were considerably longer on the road, owing to its heavy condition, and the overcrowding, almost to a suffocating point, of the vehicle: built to accommodate six inside, it was supposed to have an elastic internal capacity of its own, to which no regular rule or limit seemed to be applied; nevertheless, having in mind the more aggravated *inferno* of the stage between Council Bluffs and Savanna, I must not be too hard on this line, which, on the whole, did its work very fairly.

Omaha, it must be recollected, is the metropolis of Nebraska territory, and though now comparatively insignificant in point of size and numbers, bids fair, from its position and commercial advantages, to attain considerable importance: the last place of any size on the Missouri, save " Sioux city," it draws the trade of the river to it, while as an outfitting point for the western country it offers great advantages to freighters. But it is as the terminus of the Pacific Railroad that Omaha "hails in her heart the triumph yet to come," and begins to reckon the wealth which, as the *entrepôt* for the river trade, and the connecting link between the Eastern and Western States, must flow into her coffers. It is said that this great line is positively to run from Omaha to Denver, along the Platte valley; and the town had just been illuminated in honour of this great event, forming, as it probably will, an epoch in her history. The streets, like those of most young American "cities," are ambitiously wide, even to dreariness, and like those of Washington, were painfully ignorant of the arts of the pavior and macadamizer; the consequence was that, a hard frost supervening on heavy mud, they presented the appearance of chronic "plough," and seemed likely to remain in that state till spring.

A steam ferry-boat (now, however, frozen in) takes passengers over to Council Bluffs, in Iowa, a town deriving its name from the bluffs, which rise some five or six miles from the eastern bank of the river, pointing out the old course of this great river in clear characters. It is about the same in size, and, I should think, in numbers as Omaha; and here you take the coach for Savanna, a town connected by rail with St. Joe. Of that trajet I fear to speak, lest my memories of discomforts and hardships should

actually run away with my pen ; I will only say that
in much travelling experience over roads of most
kinds, I never met worse " going," or a line much
worse regulated. On two occasions the drivers who
ought to have " worked" us along, were so hopelessly and helplessly pantegruelistic, that their place
had to be taken by others, and the coach so over-
flowed that the passengers had to charter a waggon,
at their own expense, to get over a part of the road
till a second coach could be procured !

The country through which we passed was for
the most part undulating and well wooded. The
farms seemed comfortable, and Linden and Glyn-
wood appeared really above average specimens of
American towns of similar importance ; but of the
road I cannot speak highly, and one bridge over
which we were desired by the driver to walk, appeared
to me to be a perfect pass of peril, so completely had
the supporting framework wandered from the perpendicular.

Arrived at St. Joe, after spending twelve weary
hours in the " cars," we were informed that the road
was so blocked up by recent snow that progress was
impossible. And thus we were detained four or five
days in this very uninteresting and uninviting " city,"
in which I had already had so wearying a stay, while

waiting in vain for the "up river" boat last May. During this detention there were only two instances of "killing:" two soldiers giving each other the "happy despatch" with knives; and as the number was five in my former sojourn, I naturally formed a rather fearful opinion of the homicidal tendencies of the place.

A compulsory stay in a frontier town of even such proportions as St. Joe, leaves but few reminiscences of a pleasurable nature, to a European traveller at any rate. It is true that in the huge hotel of the place you will find, only on a much lower scale, all the comforts and plenty which you will have provided for you in one of the magnificent palaces which stud New York, and most of the principal large cities on this continent. A barber with considerable dexterity in manipulation will do his spiriting very gently on any portion of your "os sublime," to which you may direct his ministering fingers. Cunning cock-tails, or "rooster narratives," are gained by a descent of very few steps. Billiards and the dailies of many a town, with a limited supply of popular novels, are equally accessible; and, I believe, a promenade of a very mild old gentlemanly distance, will procure you all that civilized man is supposed to want, from baby-linen to a shroud, close by, if not actually in, the building where you live, move, and have your being.

Yet, in spite of this very extensive programme, which apparently leaves so little to desiderate, I know few more wearying places than such caravanserais; few where nervous sensitive temperaments are more continually blessés. And the cause lies not in any incivility on the part of employés—who, if coloured citizens of African descent, or unbleached Americans, generally set an example to their white confrères worthy of all imitation; nor yet in the accommodations, which are spacious and handsome, if bordering sometimes on the tawdry and the vulgar —but in the impossibility of escaping from the multitudinous guests, and enjoying anything approaching to quiet and repose.

Go where you will, you will find the same type of heavy, well-fed, uninteresting and unsociable beings, oppressive alike in their silence and their speech, dressed mostly in the same style, deviating but slightly from that of a respectable but second-rate undertaker: for black is an emblem of social worth in some estimations. Their personal ornamentation consists generally of a blaze of diamonds set in deep blue enamel, inserted midway in the snowy bosom of a spotless shirt (or dickey); and, if the taste be rather florid than severely "American-classic," of a ring of the same precious stone or stones. The plethora of so much unanimated broad-cloth sitting, lounging, loafing, drinking, and expectorating all around, becomes positively nightmarish, and I confess that, inhospitable as the weather was, and deep as the half-trodden snow lay on the pavés, I turned to them to get rid of the worthy occupants of the public rooms, and found a pleasant contrast in the tinkling of the many-belled sleighs which were running merrily through the streets, reminding one of the musical lines of Edgar Poe on the subject. Individually I am sure that many of these gentlemen were not only commercially estimable, but shining lights likewise in the more contracted social circle; collectively, however, to me they were simply oppressive, and I would be sorry to have to repeat my sojourn at the Pacific Hotel.

Most of these men were pig-jobbers—I use the word respectfully, for pig-jobbing has capitals such as Chicago and Cincinnati, and many another fine town in its interest—and, like myself, had been detained *malgré;* but, besides loss of time and detention, they were suffering heavily in the nightly losses of multitudes of fine fat hogs, from the great severity of the season; and yet these depletions of the pocket seemed to have no visible effect on their armour of self-complacent stoicism! Had they been loud in their denunciations of anything, or anybody, I could have felt an interest in their position, perhaps have sympathized with them; but this wall of phlegmatic impassibility was not, I felt, to be surmounted by any ladder within my reach, and as they scarcely communed with each other, I could not hope that any overtures I could make would be effective, since even the insinuating influences of " Boürbon " and " old rye " had failed to penetrate a joint in their harness.

True, there was the military element; but as the latter was drawn from much the same sources, and had grown up with much the same habits of thought and action, it diversified the scene but little, save in the matter of uniform : this was a slight relief at any rate. But here—as everywhere on this continent, so far as I have seen—the volunteer officer is not as in Europe a speciality—the representative of a class distinct from the mass of men in bearing, air, and general deportment; but, like a groom impressed on a sudden emergency to do footman's work, his livery sits ill on his unset frame, and betrays the " Pekin " at every turn : though, to their credit, I must say they do not affect the swagger so

common to "plungers," and even "red and black"
soldiers on our side of the water; as might have
been expected in men raised often from obscurity to
positions of importance and much pecuniary value,
and which, indeed, many of these men might assume
on the strength of the service they, or their regiments
at any rate, have seen, if still young in years.

However, as comparisons between volunteers in St.
Joe and European officers are perfectly irrelevant to the
Rocky Mountains and the ways thither, and as much
has been already pertinently remarked by travellers on
these and other cognate subjects, I will no longer
dwell on such topics, and as I have—maugre much
detention, and more perturbation of spirit from the
laryngial chorus sung incessantly by the expecto-
rants in the cars, whose name is not legion, but
"omnes" (the directors should provide one small
car for non-chewers, or at least furnish the others
with scuppers and swabs)—not only penetrated as far
east as Chicago, but returned again to St. Louis,
to await the arrival of my baggage; for the detention of
which the snow and storms are said to be responsible
(I would I could fix them with it); I will no longer
request the patient reader (if such I have been fortunate or unfortunate enough to find) to accompany me
further eastwards, but will pass on to a few practical

observations, which may be of service to any of my countrymen whom adventure, the love of travel, or a speculative and enterprising disposition, may tempt to explore the remote confines of "the Great West"— the proud title by which the states north-west of Virginia, who once owned most of them, are generally hailed by their eastern sisterhood.

CHAPTER V.

On ne s'embarque point sans son biscuit.—*French Proverb.*

FEW are fortunate enough, or wise enough, to finish any enterprise or expedition, the nature of which is not quite understood at the start, without feeling that were they to begin afresh there would be much of alteration and amendment attempted in the second effort to carry out their views; and my experience as to this tour has fully verified this somewhat trite and platitude-like remark. Looking back on my trip to *the* Mountains—the Rocky Sierra being the only possible candidate here for the definite article—I cannot regret my method of locomotion, though only a humble waggon, nor the companions with whom I made the passage; as the former is decidedly the best suited for seeing the country comfortably, though somewhat tedious, and apt to remind one of the "Tarda Eleusinæ matris volventia plaustra," while

the latter proved full of geniality and good-fellowship.

But, as the second contingency was a happy acci-
dent, and did not repeat itself when wanted on another
occasion, I would suggest that the first step for
travellers over "the Plains" is to secure, first, one
or more pleasant companions; next, a waggon and
team of mules or horses, as fancy may dictate: the
former I think decidedly preferable, as—if chosen
with tolerable care, and some regard to action—they
will prove better servants on the plains, *me judice*,
than horses of the same calibre, generally out-walk-
ing them—a cardinal point; and if required to trot
with a load, feeling it less than the latter; besides,
they are more marketable, and, if kept in reasonable
flesh, will sell for a figure little under or over your
purchase-money, after they have served your purpose. Indeed, both horses and mules, but especially the latter, if sold at the Rocky Mountains, will
generally realize a profit sufficient to cover a large
share of the item " contingencies."

This want will be readily supplied at any town on
the frontier, such as " Aitchison," " Leavenworth,"
" Omaha," or " Plattsmouth," and as a waggon and
team are articles of daily merchandise, but little
fluctuation occurs in their price. Indeed, there is

16—2

this remarkable difference between buying quadrupeds in England and America, and especially in
these Western States, that whereas in England,
fancy, and certain peculiarities in the animal, make
an enormous difference in the scale of valuation, in
America, as a rule, such specialities are seldom considered much in appraising the price.   The traveller
may, therefore, proceed to purchase his animals with
tolerable confidence, if he knows what he wants himself when he sees it, and has some slight experience
of draught animals ; nor need he feel painfully conscious or apprehensive that there is a screw loose
somewhere which he can only discover when hard
work begins to tell its tale, or extra pressure reveals
eccentricities of temper, or a soft place unsuspected
before.

As every one has his own ideas—or affects to have,
which comes to much the same thing—respecting horseflesh, in which I include muleflesh likewise, I will not attempt to give any hints on this
subject; contenting myself with remarking that age
is honourable in mules—if fresh in limbs and constitution—though not in horses, and that I have
generally found small, junky mules of good substance,
and standing on short legs, far more enduring than
their larger and longer-limbed brethren.   The selec-

tion of a waggon will depend so entirely on the weight to be carried, that I can only recommend the buyer invariably to go to the best maker in the place, take his advice in the matter, and not be tempted to close with any specious second-hand bargains, however tempting; as a break-down *en route* is not only vexatious, but very expensive and disagreeable.

I am assuming the case of a party of at least two, though a larger number is certainly preferable, if less manageable; but if the dual be preferred it will be found expedient to retain the services of some competent person who has been often over the line to be travelled, knows the proper stations, where water and grass are plenty and where scant, and who adds to such knowledge a limited skill in such cookery as the plains require. Such men are easily picked up on the border, as the life has great charms for these restless western spirits; and a small per-centage beyond the current wages—say twenty-five dollars per month, which, with exchange at 1·52 dollars, is not high for America—ought to secure a good " waggon-master," as he will probably style himself.

I must, however, warn my imaginary tourists that this man will have to be treated not only as their guide, but, to a certain extent, as their philosopher and friend; for though he accepts their honorarium, the teamster would not for a moment submit to be put on the footing of a servant, as we understand the term. Indeed I must say, from my experience in the West, that if you start by respecting and treating as equals the men with whom you come in contact, your own social position will be all the more fully recognized, and full credit will be given for any adventitious superiorities you may possess in rank, fortune, or education. If, however, more service be required than this, I would recommend my friends to bring a reliable man from England with them—an expensive and somewhat hazardous experiment; or, better still, to hire a negro cook and driver, with which class the country now swarms : many of whom, if closely interrogated as to antecedents, will tell you that they did not run away from their masters, but did " some mighty tall walking."

The stores of comestibles that will be required for the trip are all purchaseable at the point of departure, at rates very little, if at all, higher than if you brought them yourself from Chicago or St. Louis, and equally good ; as the market is steady, owing to the constant demand : I mean your flour, bacon, coffee, sugar, dried apples, peaches, and other fruits and berries, which ought, " de rigueur," to be included in any outfit. But, if not a teetotaller, be sure to lay in your supplies of a potable character at St. Louis ; if, indeed, you do not bring them with you from the East, where price and quality will be a point in your favour generally. The quantity necessary to take will be told you with tolerable accuracy at the place where you make your purchases ; but, as in riding over the flat, or across country, it is well to have a few pounds " in hand " for such casual contingencies as meeting Indians, or accidental delays ; for, though you can buy necessaries at the ranches, it is far better and more economical to be independent of them.

Buffalo-robes, india-rubber blankets, *et toute cette boutique*, can be got whenever you outfit ; but as airbeds and pillows are great luxuries, and pack easily, they had better be brought with you from New York.

On the subject of arms and ammunition I will be reticent, as those who would undertake such a trip will be sure to know far more than I can tell them on this head ; but I feel bound to caution others where I broke down myself ; and, in the first place, would strongly recommend shot-guns to be brought. Western men are so accustomed to the rifle from boyhood, that in many cases they know no other arm ; but it is needless to say how poor a substitute for

a shot-gun a rifle proves, even in good hands, where
small game is abundant, as it is in many parts of
the plains and mountains: besides, I much question whether at short range a Purdey or Moore would
not give as good an account of an antelope or deer,
with the aid of an Eley's cartridge, as an ordinary
rifle.   But whatever guns you bring, be sure to take
them with you from the old country, as well as
a liberal supply of ammunition: excepting powder,
which you will get of the best quality as you go
along; and fail not to recollect every implement
necessary for your shooting irons, as I found everything of that sort extremely dear and bad in the
mountains, and I lost much game, I'm sure, from
the indifferent "equipage" I procured in Denver
at a ruinous price.

I have not said a word anent saddlery, though
it is no unimportant item in an outfit: in this
case, I would advise the tourist to buy whatever he
wants in St. Louis, and not to bring his gear from
England with him.   The Californian or Mexican
saddle is peculiarly fitted for the work for which it
is meant, including packing game, and carrying your
shooting and camp necessaries, and has the rare
advantage of standing any amount of knocking about
almost with impunity.   After half an hour's riding

the body adapts itself to its uncouth-looking seat and strange wooden stirrups; and by-and-by one begins to think it actually comfortable. The M'Clellan modification of this saddle is very useful to the hunter: though in these troubled times a special permit for such a saddle is required from the provost-marshal of the district, otherwise it would probably be seized as Government property; but before starting, a document from this functionary authorizing you to carry arms generally, is indispensable, and can readily be procured.

Mentioning saddles before horses or ponies seems like putting cart before horse, but I omitted the shooting-pads, when so busy about the mules just now. In this case I would buy slowly, picking up an animal as I went along when the occasion offered, and a fair trial was possible. Indian ponies, when corn-fed and cared for, make excellent hardy animals for your purpose, and are generally very docile and handy for shooting. They can be bought generally from the ranchemen, who have probably got them at nominal figures from the Indians in the way of barter: and should you meet with a tribe of Indians, a good "truck" can often be made with them for a comparatively small supply of sugar and flour.

Some little manœuvring is, however, very necessary in trading with the Indians for horseflesh,
as they are generally no mean judges, and are not
one whit behind the pale-faced dealers in their efforts
to palm off their Leahs for Rachels; keeping their
best out of sight first, as my good friends, the
dealers "d'outre mer" will try to stick a "Flat-
catcher" into you, before they will order anything
of real "quality" to be stripped.

Having given these few, and I hope not imper-
tinent hints on the subject of preliminary preparations, I will add a word about that most important
consideration, "cost." This, though generally fore-
most in most people's minds in their estimates of
projects of either business or pleasure, is euphuis-
tically kept studiously in the background, like the
postscript of a young lady's letter in the days when
the young "Mees Anglaise" was not quite so well
posted as she is now generally supposed to be, and
actually is, in this decade of the century.

A waggon, with its full apparatus of covers, boxes,
&c., costs from 100 to 120 dollars; harness for a
pair of mules or horses about 30 or 40 dollars; while
horses—considerably raised in price by the exigencies
of the Federal War-Office, and the unprecedented
number of remounts necessitated by mismanage-

ment — can be bought from 120 to 150 dollars apiece : mules of good quality being somewhat higher.

A tent will be considered a necessary by some, and not by others, and I confess I hold rather to the latter opinion ; natheless, in wet weather, it has its advantages, and gives more room than the bed of a waggon for a dormitory : but as wet days are quite exceptional in the travelling season, and shelter is generally procurable at no very remote distance, I would feel much inclined to dispense with it as an encumbrance, where economy of space is so essential. This is an article which could be procured much cheaper in England than America, and, if insisted on, should be brought thence.

It will be perceived that I have made my estimate upon the supposition that money is an object ; but if the visitors to the Plains belong to the class to whom, in the language of the advertisements, " money is not so much an object as a comfortable home," I can assure them that the artificers in St. Louis have resources enough, at very short notice, to minister to their requirements with admirably-made spring " ambulances," contrived to serve for a bed at night as well as a chariot by day ; and also with other appliances for " doing " the Plains in an easy, com-

fortable fashion.   As, however, this style of locomotion requires what a Mr. Partington of my acquaintance calls a "revenue" of servants, and as a certain
pomp and flourish of trumpets is implied by thus
invading the desert " en milor Anglais," which never
fail to enhance prices, I have not considered the
subject in this light; but will content myself with
observing that even thus, a longer tour can be made
at cheaper rates than is possible in any country I
have ever heard or read of (Africa affords no fair
parallel), as your " stock in trade," if sold in a
more westerly market than it was bought in, will
generally realize a good profit, and even, if brought
back to its point of departure, will fetch a very fair
second-hand price; and the expense of living on the
Plains will prove the merest bagatelle.

The selection of a route or tour, when once preliminary arrangements are completed, is so entirely
a matter for private judgment and controlling circumstances, that nothing can be said pertinently in the
way of suggestion, hint, or recommendation.

Once a party is supplied with the necessary means
of locomotion and subsistence, and a guide in the
shape of some one of experience to direct proceedings, all the points of the compass, save those
belonging to the Orient, are open to them; and

their charter is not limited to a single port. Game is abundant in almost every direction; though, of course, local circumstances, only to be learned on the spot, will make animals affect particular districts at particular times and seasons. But, as a rule, it will be found that after getting out to a distance of between two and three hundred miles from the frontier, large game will show in considerable force, and good hunting will be gained by deviating a very few miles from the track of waggons and the emigration; while prairie chickens will be found in great numbers all along the settlements following the wake of corn: ducks, plover, and rabbits, will assist in making a variation in your bag, and—better still, where shooting must be "pot-hunting"—in your cuisine.

The journey overland to San Francisco *viâ* Salt Lake, is only a matter of time, as during the open weather there is not a single difficulty to overcome; and with fair management, and a few "lay overs" on Sundays, and other "jours de fête," the animals ought to look in quite as good working trim as when they started, so easy is the grading of the road, and so bountiful is the prairie generally in its stores of sustenance for all herbivorous creatures!

Between Denver and Salt Lake there is a fair chance

of meeting cinnamon or grisly bear in the pineries,
and I confess I have almost enough of the Nimrod
element in my composition to be willing to go all
the way there for a fair fight in the open with one
of the latter monsters, whose strength, size, and
ferocity forms a large share of every hunter's budget.
"He laughs at scars that never felt a wound," is, I
know, as true an aphorism now-a-days as it was in
Romeo's ; but this wise saw notwithstanding, I must
still enter my protest of incredulity about the great
danger of a passage at arms with the grey bruin, if
the hunter be only really well armed, and the ground
and surroundings be not too unfavourable. For, in the
first place, out of a number of hunters whom I have
met, I have not found or heard of more than one or
two, at least in these parts, who had suffered in the
flesh from such a battle : (one of these men had a
most ghastly witness of the puissance of a bear's
fore-arm in the loss of nearly one side of his face,)
and I have seldom, if ever, heard of " Ursa major "
or " minor " commencing an attack voluntarily on the
hunter. Wounded or brought to bay, they would, of
course, be very formidable ; but I think the chief
source of danger has consisted in the small bores of
the rifles used hitherto by the hunters, which exas-
perate without effectually stopping or maiming, as an

ounce ball from a Paton rifle is sure to do; and as a muzzle-loading rifle takes some time in the best of hands to prepare for action, the situation of the hunter, whether "tree'd" or on "terra firma," may become very parlous indeed. In the Sierra Nevada, where the grislies attain their grandest proportions, I am told the hunters prefer a double shot gun of great calibre, reserving their second charge for very close quarters.

Besides this prospect of game, there is some fishing to be had in the Platte waters; though "cat-fish" sometimes of very large size will be the staple here. But as soon as the Rocky Mountain spurs are reached first-rate trout-fishing may be obtained in almost every stream the travellers pass, if not polluted by mining operations, which banish trout as effectually as flax culture does in the North of Ireland. I found splendid sport in "the Grand" which flows through the middle park to the distant Pacific, though my success in catching large fish was not at all equal to that of many others I heard of; my largest fish not exceeding four pounds, while trout of seven and eight are no phenomena.

Were I again to find myself in that part of the country, I should not fail to try the upper waters of the "Rio Grande," which rise in some high land south of Denver, and flow on to the Gulf of Mexico, as the trout-fishing there is said to be unsurpassable ! Trust not, however, to the resources of the country for tackling, as I did, but bring everything, even a spare top or two, with you from home, as hardwood sells in the mountains for almost its weight in silver : I have to this day a lively recollection of having to disburse seven shillings for a most unartistic hickory top-joint, and glad to get it " at that." Flies, too, are very dear, fetching from one shilling to one shilling and eightpence apiece for the better sort.

But if this entire country is eminently interesting to the tourist who likes to see the varying phases of untrammelled nature, ere man with his pitchfork has tried to expel her,* or divert her into particular channels and grooves, how much more so must it be to that large class whose hearts are bigger than their means, and who crave for a field where sordid toil may be sweetened by the *zest* of excitement, and where, if there are many blanks, there are also prizes within reach.

I do not mean to say that, from what I have seen of Colorado, I would recommend it as a good field for a miner, or for an inexperienced man who wished

* Naturam expellas furcâ, tamen usque recurret.

to commence mining on his own account with but little capital, save his own labour! That stage of Colorado's development has passed, as most of the "proved" gulches have been well searched already; and the chief interest now lies in the lodes discovered in all directions, which nearly all pay well, but require some, in many instances much, capital to work effectually. Further to the north, however, in the territory of Idaho, discoveries of the richest gulches have been made within the last two years, and numbers who went there nearly as poor as Sir Walter Scott's ideal happy Irishman (see his "Song of the Shirt") have returned with fair fortunes: indeed so flattering have been the accounts, that an enormous "stampede" will probably take place in that direction in the early spring. Bancroft Library

In the south-western part of New Mexico the dreams of the old Spaniards seem to be on the point of realization in the wonderful wealth of the "dry diggings" in Arizona, as reported by men, such as clergymen located there, whose authority ought to be considered reliable. A considerable emigration will probably set in there also next spring, but not so large as towards the northern mines; for, in Arizona, the golden apples are watchfully guarded by dragons, in the shape of a civilized

17

but fierce tribe of Indians, yclept "Navajos," whom
tradition declares to be descended in part from
a Dutch colony who tried to settle near the gulf,
but were hunted into the interior by the jealous
Spaniards, to fall into the hands of the Indians, who
are supposed to have killed the men and appropriated
the female element for squaws. Certain it is that
this tribe is rich in flocks and herds and agricultural
products, while in the manufacture of blankets they
may be said to have distanced competition; a Na-
vajo blanket commanding sometimes as high a price
as one hundred dollars, from its wearing qualities,
and being impervious to water. The New Mexicans
use them commonly instead of a bucket to draw water
from a well!

This tribe, which has, I believe, gained quite a
moral ascendency over its degenerate neighbours in
New Mexico, has always resisted foreign or white en-
croachments as jealously as the Prince of Satsuma
himself; and though the United States have planted
outposts in their territories for the protection of white
men, there is still much risk from mining there, save
in parties large enough to overawe the natives!

I have already, I think, mentioned meeting English miners in Colorado; but for one Englishman
there are ten Irish at least, and the ear catches

strangely enough, amid the Teutonic and other in-
flections of harsh voices, nearly all the notes with
which it has been familiar in the diapason of brogue-
dom. One of these Milesians—and, as he has done
much good in developing the country, and giving
employment, let me name "Pat Casey"—who certainly was not born great, and would probably have
had some trouble in achieving it, has, nevertheless,
had the greatness of fortune thrust upon him, in
spite of a series of blunders enough to swamp any
enterprise!

Any one who has visited these regions will cease to
wonder at the exodus from Ireland which still goes
on, in spite of the wars and rumours of wars on this
continent. For, on the whole, labour in the mines—
if injurious to health, and even in some cases dangerous—cannot be fairly said to be hard, while the
wages are extremely good; the position of the
labourer is almost as good as that of the capitalist
or "big bug" in the social hierarchy, and the
creature comforts he enjoys transcend the wildest
hopes he ever formed in his own green isle.

In travelling I have frequently had occasion to stop
at the only inn or boarding-house of the locality,
where all, labourers and "bosses," eat together;
indeed, save in a few places where "style is put

on," this is the invariable rule observed. As breakfast is a fair sample meal, I may give an idea of what
I generally found on the table. Coffee—but very
innocent of that precious berry—will be the liquid,
with good fair sugar, and generally an accompaniment of milk. Then relays of soda rolls, hot from
the oven, will alternate with pancakes or buckwheat
cakes, eaten with butter or molasses, or maple sugar
syrup, or that of the "sorghum" cane, now so exten-
sively used westwards. There will generally be more
than one kind of hot meat, though it may consist
only in variations of pork; and lastly, sweetmeats of
some kind will flank the matutinal board, whether in
the shape of stewed apples, or peaches, or "pies,"
whose pastry requires a miner's powers of digestion,
not to speak of such small "deer" as cakes and
gingerbread in profusion.

But besides mining, there are numberless avenues
open to tradesmen and artificers in these young com-
munities, and the maxim which is so true in elder
civilizations, that "a little knowledge is a dangerous
thing," fails here altogether in its applicability. To
the farmer, too, this great West offers enormous
temptations: I mean to the man whose capital is
probably far too small to embark successfully in farming in Great Britain, but who can command a few

hundreds or even as much as a thousand pounds. Such a man may find any number of "semi-improved" farms, partially fenced, and with wooden houses and offices on them, at his disposal for a small price, varying from 80*l.* to 200*l.*, with a right of grazing over thousands of acres of good prairie-land, where his horned stock and sheep will increase and multiply his capital invested in them in a marvellous way ; for green crops here are as unknown as un-necessary, and hay, which the prairie yields freely, is all the "wintering" required for your animals.

It is certainly true that on these outlying farms cereals cannot be grown with any great profit, owing to the distance from a good market; but this does not apply to stock, for which buyers will always be glad to come, while the wool-clip can easily be stored from year to year till a tempting market offers itself. Land, indeed, in the far West can be got by simply staking out a plot of 160 acres, then recording your "claim," and making the few improvements required by law to prevent its being "jumped" in your absence. But the remarks I made had reference to farms already either purchased from the United States Government at the fixed price of five shillings per acre, or from the holders of land-warrants, or acquired under the homestead law, which makes a continuous residence of five years a good title to a holding of 160 acres; and such farms the owners — ever anxious to go further West—would be generally found willing to part with much under their value, if they estimated their own labour at current rates.

The alienage laws of the Western States—framed with a view of offering the most enormous inducements to foreigners to come and people their rich deserts, and. develop their resources—have been the means of presenting a very curious anomaly in these troublous times: aliens who have been living for years in these border States, now come forward *en masse* to claim exemption from all military service, as citizens of other countries, and bound by other allegiance; and unless their claims have been vitiated by voting, or other overt acts of United States citizenship, the Federal Government is bound to recognize their validity; if, indeed, existing laws and contracts, and the constitution of sovereign states be allowed to weigh against the more popular theories of centralization and military necessity.

In this the Western States departed widely from the more sectarian and narrow views of their Eastern sisters, which as a rule allowed none but citizens to hold real estate within them; but then the necessities of the former were more imperious, and con-

sequently the liberality of their bids for population had to rise in proportion : indeed, I think
the 'concession was rather extorted "ex necessitate
rei" than dictated by a generous comprehensive
policy. For the American *proper* is anywhere and
everywhere proud of his *descent*, and from that
height looks down on the foreigner, be he Dutch
or Irish, as his hewer of wood and drawer of water;
and if Mackintosh's much-quoted saying about
popular and national songs be true, I may, perhaps,
be pardoned for illustrating my text by the following
verse, which expresses very coarsely a state of sentiment I fear not uncommon :—

> If I were the President of the United States
> I'd frame my laws according ;
> The niggers I'd sell ; the Dutch I'd send to h—ll,
> And the Irish to the other side of Jordan.

With regard to the time required to reach the Rocky
Mountains from England, I may remark that the
postmarks on letters—better guide than any tell-tale
itineraries, or splendidly mendacious railway tables—
spoke, if I mistake not, of a term of twenty-one days
to and fro. And as no extraordinary efforts are made
to expedite the mails on this side of the Atlantic, I
have no doubt a tourist, if so minded, and of sufficiently iron constitution, could make a neck and neck

race with a letter to Denver, or even to San Francisco. But as this idea is more American than English, I will allow six weeks for reaching Denver, by which time most cities intervening, and objects of interest and curiosity can be seen; then, if the traveller be energetic, he can gain a very good idea of Colorado by a stay of six weeks, and return to England in another five weeks, including a few days for a buffalo hunt in the neighbourhood of Fort Kearney; thus accomplishing the entire tour in about four months, while the entire cost, if no accidents occur, ought to be within 200*l.*

To enjoy the expedition, however, to the fullest extent, the method I have pointed out should be adopted, in its main features at any rate; and I will venture to prophesy that if any *flaneur* in London who is weary of the perfumed airs of Bond Street, and has lost his taste for moors and stubbles, will cross the plains, and pay the Rocky Mountains a visit, he will return with a keener zest for the pleasures of civilized life, and with his "mens sana in corpore sano" all the fresher for what he has seen and experienced.

THE END.

London: Smith, Elder and Co., Little Green Arbour Court, Old Bailey, E.C.